"I'll Help You Get Warm, If You'll Let Me."

He lay down beside her and took her in his arms. Still she was shivering.

"It would be better, darling, if we had both blankets around the two of us. We could hold each other body to body—for the heat."

"You . . . you know what will happen. . . ."

He lifted her chin so that he could look into her eyes. "I know."

She could feel her anger at him give way. There in the boat, curtained by rain, they could make their own private world. Nothing that had happened before or would happen after needed to matter.

SUZANNE CAREY

is a reporter by training, a romance writer by choice, and likes to research her stories carefully and write about the places and people she knows best. For this reason, her books have a real-life quality that intrigues readers as much as it touches their hearts.

Dear Reader:

SILHOUETTE DESIRE is an exciting new line of contemporary romances from Silhouette Books. During the past year, many Silhouette readers have written in telling us what other types of stories they'd like to read from Silhouette, and we've kept these comments and suggestions in mind in developing SILHOUETTE DESIRE.

DESIREs feature all of the elements you like to see in a romance, plus a more sensual, provocative story. So if you want to experience all the excitement, passion and joy of falling in love, then SILHOUETTE DESIRE is for you.

> Karen Solem
> Editor-in-Chief
> Silhouette Books

SUZANNE CAREY
Leave Me Never

Silhouette Desire
Published by Silhouette Books New York
America's Publisher of Contemporary Romance

Silhouette Books by Suzanne Carey

Kiss and Tell (DES #4)
Passion's Portrait (DES #69)
Mountain Memory (DES #92)
Leave Me Never (DES #126)

SILHOUETTE BOOKS, a Division of Simon & Schuster, Inc
1230 Avenue of the Americas, New York, N.Y. 10020

ISBN: 0-671-49585-2

First Silhouette Books printing March, 1984

10 9 8 7 6 5 4 3 2 1

America's Publisher of Contemporary Romance

Printed in the U.S.A.

1

~~~~~~~~~~~~~~~~~

hat made you decide to come back here, anyway?
With the Moreau money, you could have gone off to
Europe if you chose."

Terry felt a tingle of the apprehension that had
plagued her on and off for weeks. She knew her friend,
Lynsley Carleton, had sensed it, and had been eagerly
waiting to question her ever since they'd talked on the
phone a few days before.

She wasn't about to satisfy Lyn's curiosity, though—
at least not yet. Her friend's brother, Jamie, was
approaching, a gin and tonic for each of them in his
hands.

With a nod in Jamie's direction, Terry stretched out
her long, shapely legs to the warm Florida sunshine,
letting the breeze off picture-postcard Coffee Pot Bayou
ruffle her short blond hair. Her skin was pale from the
Chicago winter, and now that she was going to be

working in the field again at Larsen Park Station, she would do well to get started on a tan at her earliest opportunity.

Then she made a wry face, though the expression in her large brown eyes was unreadable behind her dark glasses. That's right, she thought, stick to practical things. Here on the Carletons' palm-shaded patio, it should be easy enough to confine her thoughts to not getting sunburned, and the routine of studying and working as a biologist again. Easier than she might find it when she came face to face with Ben.

Just to be here, so close to him again, was enough to set her pulse racing. She felt an almost overwhelming need to rest her gaze on those broad shoulders of his, the dark, too-curly hair, which she knew would be threaded faintly now with silver.

Involuntarily, her lips parted at the thought of his dark-fringed blue eyes. For her, at least, those eyes would be hard and uncompromising and cold.

Jamie handed her one of the pale, lime-freshened drinks with a flourish, giving the other to his sister almost as an afterthought. A few years younger than Terry, he had always been a little in love with her. Now that she was back in Florida, he had already invited her to visit Lyn and him at their weekend home on Sanibel Island.

"Thanks," she told him with what she hoped was clearly sisterly affection. "You're a scholar and a gentleman."

He grinned. "My pleasure. I'll just get my own drink and be back in a flash."

But Lyn wasn't about to give up her chance for a *tête-à-tête*. "Not on your life, little brother," she said. "This time, it's just womantalk."

With a shrug of disappointment and a casual "See

you at dinner," Jamie headed back toward the big stucco house.

"Now," said Lyn, leaning forward a little. "I want the truth."

Again Terry hesitated. "I suppose it was seeing Ben on television," she admitted finally, thankful for the camouflaging sunglasses.

"Ah, so you caught the Bob Doherty show. I wondered."

Terry had "caught" the show, all right; or rather, it had caught her—unawares. Lonely and at loose ends after Philip's death, she had flipped on the popular talk program one morning, only to find herself looking into Ben's eyes. Mouth dry and knees quaking, she had sunk down on the couch before the set. Ben had been discussing his astonishing new book, *The Urge to Love*.

"There's been quite a furor over that book of his," Lyn noted. "I can't believe you approve. . . ."

"I don't, really."

Like Terry's late father, Ben had always been a purist about his biology. She knew his first two books, both scientific treatises on birds, would have made Herbert Daniels proud.

But now Ben had chosen to lend his name and prestige to a popular science and self-help manual, coauthored with California psychologist Avery Wilder. The book jacket noted wryly that Wilder was known as the prophet of the "me" generation. Ben's impeccable credentials were stated without much editorial comment. And Terry had to give him credit. He *had* stuck to technical, scientific material in the chapters attributed to him.

Nonetheless, his collaboration with Wilder had earned him some frowns and raised eyebrows in the scientific community. As for Terry, the book had left her with an uneasy feeling. She imagined that she detected a thread of cynicism running through Ben's commentary. Had she permanently disillusioned him about love, then, when she had walked out on him six years before?

"Well, then?" Lyn was watching her as she sipped at her drink. "If you're not impressed, why did you let yourself in for Larsen Park again, and working under his direction for your doctorate? As I said, you have the money to do as you please. And your father was probably the most highly respected ornithologist in this country. If you must be dreary and push for another degree, you could get accepted anywhere."

Terry was silent a moment. "Ben's the best," she said. "Even if I don't always agree with him."

She didn't expect Lyn to understand. How could anyone understand the way she had felt when she'd seen him on the screen—as if she had been starving or dying of thirst. She had fed on the angles and planes of his jaw and firm profile, drunk in the hard, glittering humor of those blue, blue eyes.

"You have to give the devil his due," said Lyn. "He's as good-looking as ever."

At *least* that, Terry thought. There had been new lines in his face, of course, and premature silver strands among the unruly dark curls. He would be thirty-five now, she realized. But he hadn't really aged, just grown harder, more confidently virile, if that were possible.

A man in his prime, he would still be devastatingly attractive to women—even if he were disillusioned with them, thanks to his treatment at her hands. No celibate, he would have known many lovers since she had turned him aside.

Lyn gave a little sigh, bringing Terry's attention back to the present. "What happened between the two of you before, anyway?" she asked. "I used to get the impression you were at odds. Did you have a love affair?"

"Yes," she said softly, looking down at her hands, at the finger that until recently had been adorned with Philip Moreau's diamond. "Ben and I were planning to be married."

Quietly, Terry's friend patted her hand. Lyn might be making a career out of attending social events until she and her attorney boyfriend could be married in the fall, but she was nobody's fool. "Don't tell me if you don't want to," she said.

The shadows of the ragged tender banana leaves and cocos plumosas that fringed the patio flickered in the breeze. Terry shook her head, unwilling to dredge up her painful memories. "I'd rather not, if you don't mind," she said. "What's past is past."

There was a flurry of activity by the seawall as a neighbor docked his boat, then threw some fish to the waiting pelicans. Lost in her own thoughts, Terry plucked a hibiscus bloom that dangled within reach and then shredded it between her fingers.

Meditatively Lyn swirled the melting ice cubes in her glass. "Still, it will be a bit sticky now, won't it?" she asked. "With him as your major professor, in charge of your destiny, so to speak?"

Sticky wasn't the word. "As a matter of fact, I wasn't sure I'd be accepted," Terry said. "But then the letter came back from the dean, stating that Dr. Reno had agreed to sponsor me. I . . . suppose he did it out of obligation."

"To your father?"

"Yes." Terry tossed the bits of flower aside. "Ben always was a man who understood obligation."

* * *

Terry repeated that reasoning to herself the following afternoon as she headed out across the causeway toward the Howard Frankland Bridge, en route to Larsen Park.

Ben agreed to sponsor me for one reason and one reason only, she thought. He did it for my father, because of what they were to each other as colleagues and friends, and because my father is dead. *Not,* she reminded herself, because he wants to see me again.

The scent of the bay reached her as she hit the metal span that crossed the water's expanse, milky blue and dully sparkling in the early afternoon haze. Her route east would not take her past Florida Gulf Coast University, where Ben taught and where she was officially enrolled now to get her own advanced degree. She had seen pictures of it in the catalogue—a wide, oak-studded campus with buff brick buildings—and had been unable to imagine the man she'd once loved as a stodgy professor there.

As she drove, hot Florida sunshine poured into the open convertible and she could feel her skin burn. By the time she got to the station, she would look like a lobster. Pulling off onto the shoulder, she dabbed her nose with zinc oxide and tied on a straw hat. And now I won't think of him, she promised herself, edging back into traffic.

At ten minutes past three, she was turning down Larsen Road, past woods of sand pine that were part of the station grounds. On her right was a newly planted citrus grove, property of Victor Larsen, son of the philanthropist who had endowed Larsen Park. The huge Larsen holdings bounded the station on three sides, she recalled, while she managed the slight skid of the MG's tires in the deep sand ruts.

A moment later she was passing through the station's iron gates, driving slowly under huge moss-bannered oaks that arched over the road.

Glancing nervously in her rearview mirror, she wiped away the last traces of zinc oxide and took off her hat, running one hand through her honey-colored curls. She had gotten a sunburn despite her precautions, and she had chewed off half her lipstick. With any luck, Ben would be in the field and she would have a chance to freshen up.

The station itself still seemed a magical place. To Terry, it had always been like an island, filled with brilliant light, the quiet punctuated only by the sound of the breeze and the calls of birds and insects. Herbert Daniels had originally chosen it for the research he'd done every summer because it offered one of the few ranges left to an endangered species, the Florida scrub jay, the bird that was now Ben's life work.

Emerging from the woods, she saw the main building ahead. A vine-clad Tudor lodge with a series of attached two-story hip-roofed bays that housed the laboratories, it still looked for all the world like a railway depot there in the quiet, hot sunlight.

In fact, an infrequently used spur of the Seaboard Coast Line Railroad did run behind the building. The veranda that shaded the length of the structure like a waiting platform did nothing to dispel the depot impression.

Beyond, the scrub habitat stretched to the west. Once part of the estate of the late construction magnate Olaf Larsen, the lodge, labs and surrounding acreage were now operated by a private foundation for wildlife and native plant preservation and research.

Her heart skipped a beat as she realized that there were two men on the veranda, one of them red-haired and youngish, the other tall, broad shouldered, his hair hidden by a canvas hat.

Heavier than Ben. And fair. She let out her breath in a little rush.

She got herself in hand with difficulty, still sinkingly aware that Ben might be only a few feet away, watching her arrival from behind one of the laboratories' glass doors. As she pulled the MG slowly up to the steps, she received two friendly greetings.

"Welcome," said the older of the two men, reaching across the passenger seat to shake her hand. He was about fifty. "I'm Dave Thornton, director here. We've been expecting you, Miss Daniels."

"Call me Terry, please," she replied, smiling with more enthusiasm than she felt but liking the sandy-haired, athletic-looking Dave Thornton.

"Terry it is. I suppose you've heard this before, but I admired your father very much."

She smiled a little. "Thank you. That's always nice to hear."

The red-haired youth, probably no more than twenty or so, was grinning at her.

"Since Dr. Thornton won't introduce me, I'll take care of that myself," he said, with a keen twinkle in his green eyes. "I'm Arch VanMeter, one of your fellow sufferers under the great Dr. Reno. Welcome to the club. I must say you're a phenotypically decorative addition."

"Hi." Terry shook his hand in turn. "I'm not sure whether to feel apprehensive or complimented."

He winked at her. "Probably both would be appropriate."

Dave Thornton shook his head. "Arch *will* be arch," he said. "You'll get used to his sense of humor. Why don't you park on the other side of the turnaround, across from the garage, and Arch can get you registered, show you to your room. I'm sure you'll want to wash up before you go down to the lab to see Ben."

So he was not in the field, but nearby, as her instincts had told her.

"I would appreciate that," she said in a small voice.

Keeping up a stream of friendly chatter, Arch Van-Meter found her a registration form in the station office, and then carried her bags upstairs from the lounge to the same sparely furnished women's dormitory where she and Ben had made love six years before.

Except for some new carpeting, it hadn't changed. It still had the same monastic air, the same high windows with neat blinds and no curtains, three narrow beds with white hobnail spreads, even the remembered print of mountain sheep near the Great Divide.

To all appearances it was uninhabited. "Am I to have it all to myself?" she asked Arch, glancing around in surprise. "I thought there was at least one other female student here at the station."

"There is—Janet Vickery. She's tracking bobcats using telemetry collars. But she lives in one of the cottages with Ann Nesbitt, our housekeeper, and gets her board free by helping take charge of Ann's son Charlie. We get groups out here some weekends, as you probably remember. I imagine you'll have roommates then."

Does Ben still bunk across the hall in the men's quarters? she wanted to ask. But no, he probably used one of the cottages too, now that he had professor status.

Putting down her purse and zippered flight bag on one of the beds, she turned to face her redheaded guide.

He was watching her with a faintly rueful look of

appreciation. "You really are lovely, you know," he said. "And smart, too, I understand. Too bad that I won't stand a chance next to Dr. Reno."

Did Ben make it with all the women graduate students? she wondered uncomfortably.

A stricken look must have come over her face. "Hey," said Arch, "Ben's not so bad. I thought you knew. I understand you used to work with him."

With difficulty, she regained her composure. "It's been a long time."

"Well, fame hasn't changed him . . . much. For the worse or the better. See you downstairs. I'll walk down to the lab with you when you're ready." Giving her a little salute, Arch retreated. She could hear him whistling as he went down the stairs.

Standing there in the middle of the room, Terry let herself shake a little. Then, willing herself to be calm, she took her makeup kit and the folded towel and washcloth that had been provided, and went down the hall to the quaint, oversized communal bathroom.

With its cool, quarry tile floor, huge old-fashioned onyx-green fixtures, and the frosted crank-out window shadowed by a ficus vine, the bath had always seemed an anachronism—left over from the station's days as a private estate.

Someone, definitely male and possibly Ben, had left a bottle of aftershave on the washstand. Removing the cap, she sniffed it, finding that it had a vaguely remembered mossy scent.

I'm really here, she thought, replacing the aftershave and beginning to wash the road dirt from her face and hands. Back in his life, for better or for worse.

Ten minutes later she was walking beside Arch along the concrete veranda, trying to appear calm, but aware that her shyness and apprehension were showing a little.

Then Arch was rolling back the sliding glass door to the general lab. Along with the familiar odor of chemicals, she caught her first glimpse of the man she'd come so far to see—a man still so special and beautiful it made her heart ache to think she had turned him aside.

2

꧖꧖꧖꧖꧖꧖꧖꧖꧖

He was sitting at the big, scarred desk her father had always used, engrossed in discussion with a student.

As always, he used his hands when he talked, but with a controlled energy that was distinctly his own. Seen at close range, his hair was still outrageously dark and curly. Its faint sprinkling of silver only reminded her poignantly of the years they had lost.

Beneath his sweat-stained blue shirt, his shoulders were as broad and straight as ever. His legs, bare between cutoffs and field boots, were furred with dark hair the way she remembered, and tanned deeply by the sun.

He turned at the sound of their entrance.

"Here's the decorative addition to our crew we've been expecting," Arch said.

Terry went cold as she gazed into Ben's eyes—still bluer than blue and totally uncompromising.

The silence between them lengthened, grew awkward. She could feel Arch and the other student staring. One of us has to say something, she thought.

"Hello, Ben," she managed at last, in a voice that seemed to belong to someone else. "It's . . . been a long time."

"Six years."

The words were raspy and deep, a statement of fact, an indictment, or perhaps a warning not to intrude in his personal life again. She didn't know which, could only be certain of the tension between them.

"I'm sorry about your father," he added, his eyes still holding hers as if by magnetic force. "He meant a lot to me. I . . . was at the funeral, you know."

There was a lump, now, in her throat. "I didn't know," she said. "I'm sorry . . . I didn't get a chance. . . ."

He shrugged, glanced away, but not before she had seen the animosity in his face. It was almost as if he had said the words aloud: *It's just as well.*

"Bob," he said, turning to the beefy young man who had been sitting on the lab table beside him and had now gotten to his feet. "This is Terry Daniels . . . or is it Moreau? You put Daniels on your application."

"I've gone back to using it," she said. "I . . . guess it symbolizes my seriousness about my work."

For a moment the mask dropped again and she could see his hostility, his unwillingness to believe her. Then, "I see," he said without much expression. "Terry, this is Bob Dawes. He and Arch are studying vocalizations as predator warnings among the jays. I assume you've come back to work on a phase of the project."

"Yes," she said, self-consciously taking Bob Dawes's hand. "That's what I hope to do."

"Well, you'll have some time to decide what contribution you want to make."

Casually then, almost insolently, he let his gaze drop to her feet and travel in a blatant way the others could not mistake up the curves of her legs. His eyes continued their journey, lingering on the shape of her breasts under the faded sun top she wore. It was territory he knew all too well, if only from memory.

"I may be able to offer some suggestions," he added, again meeting her eyes.

So that's how it's to be, she thought, a combination of cold indifference and insolence. Add to that a heavy dose of skepticism about my seriousness as a scientist. He hasn't forgiven me in the slightest, not for leaving him or for letting my commitment to science lag. She longed suddenly to slap him. Or to cry.

Her chin lifted a little. "I'd appreciate any guidance you'd care to give," she said, as coldly as she dared, wanting to punish him because she would so much rather have been taken in his arms. "I realize how fortunate I am to be accepted as your student."

Ben's eyes narrowed. Here it comes, she thought. The bare truth.

He didn't disappoint her. "You had connections," he said. "And I don't mean your Moreau relatives, either. Now, if you don't mind, we'll have an opportunity to talk later. Bob and I have something to thrash out. Arch, you can stay; this concerns you too."

Her face flamed. He had dismissed her, sent her away as an outsider, a person of no importance.

Avoiding the other students' eyes, she turned and walked out of the lab without a word. It's going to be all over the station that we don't like each other, she thought. More than anything, she wanted to go upstairs, take her few belongings back to the car and drive anywhere, as long as it was away from Larsen Park.

But of course that was just what Ben expected her to do. Probably what he was hoping for. His obligation to her father would be fulfilled.

Well, I won't let him do it to me, she thought. I'm going to dig in my heels.

Thirsty, she remembered the soft-drink machine that was housed just under the porch, in the entryway to the half-basement storeroom. Making her way to the machine, she fished a quarter out of her pocket, selected a bottle of soda and carried it back out into the brilliant sunlight.

A hike in the scrub, if only a little way back, would calm her, settle her resolve. She needed a chance to absorb the station's particular brand of quiet, to feel this warm winter sun on her neck again and drink in the long, quavering trill of a pine warbler.

She knew the work itself would be deeply satisfying. She had caught her enthusiasm for the Florida scrub jay from her father, and despite her six-year absence from the project he had started, she was genuinely excited at the prospect of field study.

Just the physical exertion of counting birds, mapping territories and locating nests would be a pleasure. Surprisingly sedentary and tame, the jays could be coaxed with peanuts and would come at a whistle to sit on the researchers' fingers.

Even the grueling aspect of the labor that lay ahead would be good for her, she thought. Perhaps the hot sun, the thirst that demanded huge quantities of water and iced tea and lemonade, even the exhaustion at day's end might help her to forget her heartache over Philip's death and the mess she had made of her life.

* * *

Supper was an awkward affair, with Terry and Ben scarcely speaking to one another. Most of the station personnel were present in the long dining room. Terry met Ann Nesbitt, who was station housekeeper now, and Janet Vickery of the bobcat project. Ann, a tall, soft-spoken woman of about forty, did double duty as cook, and served up platters of Southern fried chicken, potatoes, biscuits, corn and okra, and huge pitchers of iced tea.

Unwilling to look at Ben too much, Terry concentrated on the meal. After all, like the others, she was hungry from a day spent in the out-of-doors. She trained her gaze instead on her new acquaintances.

Table talk was sparse. What conversation there was ranged from the threat of phosphate mining in the Osceola Forest to the Florida panther Janet was certain she'd spotted a few days earlier. There was a brief mention of trouble on something called the Lake Annie tract, which Terry gathered was a property adjoining Larsen Park. Curious, she held back her questions, not wanting to call attention to herself.

Finally Ann brought in dessert—calamondin pie— and then they were getting up from the table, taking plates and cutlery back to the kitchen, dispersing to their evening pursuits. Ben promptly disappeared to the lab, as did Arch and Bob Dawes. Janet drifted away somewhere.

Not wanting to intrude on anyone, but feeling lonely, out of place and at loose ends, Terry read for a while in the quiet library, wishing herself anywhere else on earth. Despite the pep talk she had given herself that afternoon, she was beginning to think it had been a mistake to come.

At about nine, she was thirsty again, and returned down the narrow steps to the soft-drink machine.

Beneath the single weak bulb that illuminated the little basement anteroom, she dug out another quarter and was about to insert it when she heard footsteps on the stair.

Arch, she thought. He'll probably want to ask me a billion questions.

Turning her back, she put in her coin, extracted the moisture-beaded bottle and removed the cap. Then something, a sixth sense perhaps, made her wheel around. She was facing, not her redheaded fellow student, but Ben.

Clearly he had not expected to bump into her in that small, intimate, poorly lit space. All the anger, the hurt, the hatred he had been holding back in their afternoon encounter were showing now in his face.

"Ben," she breathed.

"Why did you come here?" he demanded, his voice low so that no one outside would hear.

"But . . . you already know," she began lamely, suddenly afraid of the depth of feeling she could discern in him. "I . . . came to get my doctorate."

Scorn filled his words. "You could get that anywhere. There are other ornithologists with fine reputations. Why me? To rake up old memories? To see if the old spark still burns?"

"No, Ben," she lied, knowing in that instant that it *was* a lie. "You have to believe—"

"Like hell I do."

With one hand, he reached up and unscrewed the single overhead bulb with bare fingers, so that the room was thrown into darkness.

Before she could cry out or even speak, his other arm had come crushingly around her, pulling her up against the remembered male length of him.

Her nostrils filled with his heady scent even as his

mouth descended on hers in a rough, devouring, almost punishing kiss that denied her breath and sent her senses reeling.

Half a day at the station and she was back in his arms, her body knowing the way. She could feel his male desire, hard against her. Pressing close, she was unable to help what she felt.

His other hand caught at the nape of her neck, tangling in her close-cropped curls and forcing her head back so that her mouth opened to admit his tongue. But there was no tenderness in his kiss, only raw, retributive passion so bitter it resembled dislike more than affection.

Her breath returned in a soft little gasp as finally he took his mouth from hers and moved back a little to hold her tightly by the shoulders.

"Was that what you came back for?" he demanded, his low whisper full of a taut irony, almost a disgust that seemed partly directed against himself. "Did you want to prove that I still can't keep my hands away?"

"No . . . I . . ." She could feel her dismay and confusion mount as his fingers tightened, hurting her.

"Well, you have, damn you," he said, his rough voice grating in her ear. "I thought I had you out of my system, that I was immune after all these years. God knows, I've tried hard enough to be. But let me tell you something, lady. It isn't *love* that I feel for you."

Tears were streaming down her face, though she wasn't aware of them. "Don't you think I know that?" she cried, her voice shaking on the words. "After . . . after what happened, I could hardly expect you to be waiting with open arms. But I guess I *did* expect that you'd understand why I'd want to carry on my father's work. . . ."

Anger blazed up in his eyes at that, and for a moment, the silence seemed to crackle with tension.

"You're here now," he told her finally, the words flint-edged. "And you can stay—provided you do the work and don't expect any special favors. But don't invoke Herbert Daniels as your patron saint again, even if you *are* his daughter. And don't thrust your beautiful body at me as a peace offering, either. I just might take it. . . ."

Humiliation flooded her. With a little cry, she wrenched free, stumbled blindly up the dark steps into the lighted parking area in front of the veranda, clutching the all but forgotten bottle of soda in her hand.

Ben did not follow. In the woods to the east, beyond the garage and water tower, a chuck-will's-widow gave its hollow, whistling call. From somewhere, the soft chords of a guitar floated out into the cool night air.

Terry stood quite still for a moment, getting her bearings. She was still shaking. Gradually she became aware that the guitar music was coming from the far end of the porch. Janet Vickery was sitting there, alone on the step, strumming and looking her way. She nodded an invitation.

Brushing the traces of tears from her cheeks and hoping that what she was feeling didn't show very much, she walked slowly in Janet's direction. Behind her, she could hear Ben come up the steps at last. A moment later, she heard the door to the lounge close behind him.

"Be my guest," Janet said, indicating the step beside her as she picked a series of random notes between songs. "I'm giving my nightly concert—to the barred owls and squirrels. Anything wrong?"

"Not . . . really." Terry took the proffered seat.

"I saw Dr. Reno go down, and then you came running up like he had slapped you," Janet said softly. "Did he make a pass at you?"

Hardly that, thought Terry, though some might consider it so.

"We had words," she admitted. "I . . . suppose you've heard we used to work together, under my father. But we never liked each other very much."

That's true, she thought. It was never mere liking, always more or less than that.

Janet was silent a moment, lightly fingering the notes of a vaguely familiar folk melody. "Then why did you come here to study under him?" she asked.

Ben thinks he knows the answer to that, Terry said to herself ruefully. And, in a way, he's right. But I had some redeeming motives too, whatever he believes.

"I suppose because the scrub jay project was my father's first," she answered, keeping her emotions at bay. "And because Ben's good, the best in his field. I guess I knew he'd . . . have to accept me, because of my father, you know."

Removing the guitar from her lap and resting it against her knee, Janet smoothed back her nondescript ponytail with one hand. "He's good, all right," she said. "One of the best, as you say . . . even if we don't all approve of the way he teamed up with Avery Wilder to do that pop psychology book. Faculty positions at the university don't pay all that well. I suppose he did it for the money . . . and you really can't blame him."

Unaccountably, Terry found herself rising to Ben's defense. "I'm sure he believed it would be of some value or he wouldn't have done it," she said. "If money were all he cared about, he wouldn't still be here at the station, bothering about students like Arch and Bob and me, or doggedly gathering bits of data on the jays that might not form a meaningful picture for years. . . ."

She stopped, her voice trailing off in embarrassment. But Janet didn't comment on her impassioned apologia for Ben. Instead, as if the blond zoology student realized that Terry didn't want to discuss Ben any further but would turn only half an ear to any other topic, she got to her feet and bid Terry a quiet good-night.

Moving a step further into the shadows, Terry watched Janet walk along the veranda and go in by the lounge door. How I wish I could ask her why she thought Ben had made a pass at me, she admitted. Was it because he does that with all his students?

But she realized the question would have only sparked speculation on Janet's part.

In the dark, wooded area beyond the courtyard, the chuck-will's-widow called again, a mournful sound. It feels just the same here, she thought, and yet how drastically things have changed.

A movement behind her startled her, jolting her from her reverie. But it was only Arch, opening and shutting the glass doors of the general lab as he finished up for the evening.

"Going to sit there in the dark like that all night?" he called. "We can find something better to do if you don't want to watch basketball on television."

Terry shook her head. "Thanks," she said. "Not tonight. I'm about to turn in anyway."

Arch shrugged and threw her a smile. "Some other time," he said, walking off down the porch and going into the lounge.

She sat there another minute or two, swigging down the last of the soda. I might as well go to bed, she thought. I don't want to run into Ben again tonight.

He was sitting in the TV room beyond the lounge with Arch and Bob, watching the game. Unlike the others, he did not look up or say good night as she came in and went up the stairs.

The sounds from the set and the men's low comments carried faintly after her as she groped about the dark hallway and located a light switch just inside her dormitory room. They ceased as she shut the heavy door.

Standing there in the quiet, almost antiseptic room, she felt excruciatingly alone. This is worse than the Moreaus' big gray house, she thought, far worse than all the bright, desperate lies I told Philip about being content with the life we had.

Ben is here, within reach. Maybe he will even sleep across the hall. And yet he'll be a million miles away.

She was painfully aware that the narrow little bed she'd chosen was the same one they'd shared so long ago, whispering their endearments and pretending her father wouldn't guess. Thomas Wolfe said it, she thought bitterly, picking up her robe and toothbrush for the trek to the bathroom. You can't go home again.

Returning to her room, she noted the empty soda bottle, which she'd unthinkingly carried upstairs. Powerfully, the memory of Ben's kiss in the cramped basement anteroom returned, and with it the memory of an earlier time when he'd caught her half-naked with an unopened bottle of soda in her hand.

It hadn't been just an easy tumble into bed. No, Terry thought, *not that*. But there was so much tension between us, I suppose it was inevitable that we would fall in love.

It had all started the day they met, when her father had unexpectedly asked his new graduate student to stay to supper.

LEAVE ME NEVER

Ben Reno had been quite the best-looking man she'd ever seen. On impulse, Terry went to the closet that contained the few personal things she'd brought to the station and dug through a carton. A moment later, she found what she wanted—the slim leather-bound volume in which she'd recorded the events, thoughts and feelings of what now seemed the happiest days of her life. The bed springs squeaking beneath her, she settled back against her pillows and propped the diary on her knees.

3

Ben Reno is one of the most unsettling men I've ever met," she had written in a rounded, girlish hand after their initial meeting. "*Mom shooed us out on the porch after dinner, and he sat so close to me on the swing it gave me shivers. I didn't know what to say to him. Oh, I suppose I could have asked him to tell me more about himself. He had been telling us at dinner about his career in the Navy. But he didn't really give me a chance. 'You know something about me,' he said in that deep, raspy voice of his. 'Tell me about yourself.'*

"*I couldn't help noticing how good he smelled, the way his fingernails were neatly trimmed and light against the tan of his hands.*"

Terry shook her head slightly, turned a page.

"*Probably he realized I was staring. 'Aren't you going to answer me?' he asked. I told him I was going into ornithology too, that I was going to be a full-fledged field assistant to my father for the first time on the Florida project.*

"He looked at me in a funny kind of way and then picked up my left hand and examined Philip's ring. 'That's quite a chunk of diamond you're wearing,' he said. 'I take it you're engaged.'

"I admitted that was true, mentioned Philip's name. Immediately he picked up on it. 'Not of the meat-packing Moreaus, surely?' he said, raising one eyebrow in a way that was positively infuriating.

"It put me on the defensive. 'What if he is?' I said. 'He has a lot going for him besides money. He's getting his MBA. And he works.'

"The eyebrow only shot up further. 'Where?' he said. 'At one of the family plants?' I answered sharply that Philip worked in the administrative offices at Moreau Industries, and then I could have bitten my tongue, because I realized he was laughing at me. 'Of course,' he said, and his eyes were positively glinting with amusement, 'I didn't think he stood ankle-deep in the slaughterhouse.'

"Later, when Ben found out Philip would be off in Europe while I traveled to Florida with my father, he told me Philip was a fool. 'You're beautiful,' he said, 'even with that belligerent attitude. I wouldn't be so casual about things if you were mine.'"

Reading his words now, Terry could remember all too well how they had haunted her. They had even tempered her anger later, when he had cast aspersions on her dedication to science, saying that if she married Philip she'd never amount to more than a name in the social column.

I should have known then that I was in love with him, she thought. Maybe I did know it, in my secret heart. I certainly spent enough time denying it.

Meanwhile, she remembered, she had memorized nearly everything about Ben, even training her field glasses on him sometimes when he couldn't guess what she was doing. As they worked together that summer in Larsen Park, she had learned his every mannerism and gesture, and could have unerringly selected his dark head and broad set of shoulders from a cast of thousands.

But Ben had made no move as the heat settled in with a vengeance and the hatchlings they were studying fledged. The sexual tension between them stretched tauter still, snapping sometimes in little bursts of argument.

She had been at odds with him over some obscure scientific question one weekend when they all went to Sanibel Island, where her parents had rented the Carletons' cottage on the beach. Terry's mother had noticed immediately that something was wrong, and she had commented on it as she and Terry sat on the cottage steps drying their hair after a late swim. "Why don't you like Ben?" Miriam Daniels had asked. "He seems nice enough to me."

Terry had shrugged, unwilling to meet her mother's perceptive gaze. "I don't know," she'd said as listlessly as she could. "I guess I don't care for his arrogance. He's a snob about science and he acts as if I don't take it seriously."

Her mother had given her a knowing look. "He'll mellow," she had remarked indulgently. "And so will you. Somehow, I had the feeling the problem between the two of you went deeper than that."

The next day, Terry's parents had gone to Fort Myers for shopping and dinner while Ben had announced he would be working all day at the Ding Darling Wildlife Refuge on the opposite side of the island.

Thinking herself alone in the cottage, Terry had returned from a swim and stripped off the top half of her bikini before going to the kitchen for a cooling drink.

Lost in memories now of that cataclysmic moment, she gently turned her diary's faintly yellowing pages.

"Ben was standing there at the screen door," she had written, *"wearing only cutoffs and beach thongs and looking at me. His eyes seemed to rake over me. I couldn't move. A moment later, he was inside the room and his arms were around me. It was like shelter, the deepest I have ever known. When his mouth covered mine, I knew what we both wanted. There wasn't any fear.*

"At last he moved back a little, his eyes burning blue into mine, and took the cold bottle of soda I was holding between us. 'I don't want you to be thirsty when we make love,' he said, opening it. 'Go on, Terry. Drink it. Save a little for me.'"

With a little moan, Terry let the diary slip from her grasp to the hobnail spread. Her eyes shut tight, she relived the way Ben had taken a long draught of his own from the bottle, and then knelt on the linoleum to kiss her breasts.

Almost before she had realized what he was doing, he was sliding her bikini bottom from her hips. "No," she had exclaimed weakly. "You mustn't. I'm engaged. . . ."

"So?" His breath on her skin had made her shiver as he kissed the little hollows by her pelvic bones, laid his cheek hotly against her thighs. "Haven't you been wanting this too, for weeks?"

She hadn't protested again, not even when he had led her to the small, green-tiled bath and turned on the shower spray. How could she have, when he was so beautiful, kicking off his rubber thongs and unzipping his khaki cutoffs, then stepping in beside her, so big in the small space?

Afterward, on her narrow little bed, he had joined his body lovingly, oh so lovingly, to hers. The delight he had taught her then had shown her, for the first time, how far the chemistry between a man and a woman could go. He had been sweet and gruff when he finally moved off her and drew her head against his shoulder.

"With sex out of the way," he had told her, his voice warm and yet faintly mocking, "maybe we can really get to know each other."

Recalling those words, Terry hugged her pillow against herself and shut out the light.

Sunlight was flooding in between narrow blinds when she awoke the next morning. The fragments of a dream hovered hauntingly on the fringes of her consciousness. There had been something about herself and Ben—something about wedding plans. Herbert Daniels had given them his blessing.

For a moment, Terry buried her face in the pillow, shutting out emotion. Then she reached for her watch on the night table and examined it. The dial showed a quarter after eight. Below, the courtyard was empty except for Ann Nesbitt's son, Charlie, who was doing wheelies on his twenty-four-inch bike as he waited for his school bus.

Breakfast at Larsen Park was served early, about seven-thirty if the routine was still the same. Probably everyone had gone out in the field without her.

Sleeping late on your first day here is hardly the way to impress anyone with how serious you are, she reminded herself. Tossing back the covers, she went quickly to the big old-fashioned bathroom to wash and dress.

Charlie Nesbitt paused in his desultory amusement to stare at her as she emerged into the courtyard a few minutes later. "I suppose breakfast is over," she said, giving him a friendly if rueful smile. "Did everyone leave for the field?"

He nodded. "Everyone except Dr. Thornton," he said. "C'mon. My mom's still in the kitchen. She can fix you something."

Ann Nesbitt greeted Terry with a smile, readily agreeing to fix her some orange juice and several pieces of toast. Leaning against the counter and drinking a cup of coffee, Dave Thornton shook his head. "That was some snooze you had," he said. "I presume you'll be getting up earlier tomorrow, when your work here officially gets under way."

"You can count on that." Terry felt a touch of embarrassment. "I'm sorry I missed going out with the group this morning."

"They'll be back at noon. You can go out after lunch, if you want. Meantime, Arch is driving into town on some errands for me. You can tag along if you have nothing else to do."

The redheaded, voluble Arch proved glad of her company and kept up a steady stream of talk as they traversed the seven miles or so north to the small, old-fashioned citrus growers' town of Lake Placid.

Terry herself had little to say. Feeling oddly detached, she followed Arch around the local hardware store and family-owned supermarket.

At the drugstore, Arch had to order a prescription, and she strolled over to the film counter with the idea of picking up some supplies to photograph her research.

As she discussed the relative merits of two types of color film with the clerk, she found herself glancing sideways at a tall woman of about thirty who had come to stand beside her.

The woman, who was dressed in a khaki bush jacket and slim trousers, seemed interested in their conversation. With one long-fingered, gemless hand, the woman swept back her shoulder-length, straight brown hair and asked, "What are you trying to shoot? I'm something of a photographer. Maybe I can help."

Terry named the two brands of film she'd been considering, the ASA sensitivity of each, and the fact that her subject would be birds. "It's . . . been a long time, really," she said, "since I've taken any photographs at all."

The woman smiled, revealing white, even teeth and the crinkles around her greenish hazel eyes. "It's like riding a bike," she said. "It'll come back to you. I'd pick *this* kind. I like a slightly more bluish cast to my color work. The other tends to highlight yellow tones."

Terry nodded. "Light's usually pretty harsh where I'll be shooting," she said. "But I'd like some cloudy day shots, too, and evening ones. I never seem to get enough light *and* speed when I want to catch the birds in flight."

"Four hundred is fast enough. You can push the film, you know—set the ASA higher for an entire roll and get the shutter speed you want without losing your depth of field. Just tell whoever is developing your stuff, so they can compensate."

Thanking her impromptu adviser, Terry paid for several rolls and walked away to leaf through some magazines while she waited for Arch.

But the drugstore was a small place, and she couldn't help overhearing the woman ask for ten rolls of the same film she had recommended, any more than she could help turning to watch the woman go out, get into a burgundy-colored Mercedes and drive away.

The same Mercedes was parked beside the station veranda when they returned.

"Hey," said Arch as he, too, noticed the Mercedes. "Abby's back."

"Abby?" Terry questioned.

"Yeah. Abby Williams, the wildlife photographer. Her stuff's become pretty well known around Florida. I'm really glad she's here."

"Why?" Terry asked, gripped by an uneasy premonition. "Do you like her that much?"

"Not *me*," he said with a wink, "though I think she's a classy lady. It's Dr. Reno who *likes* her, if you know what I mean. Whenever she's here, he's his most gracious self, and that makes life easier on us."

Terry felt her throat tighten. This was a twist she hadn't counted on. Ben had a mistress. Of course, she'd guessed he would. But accepting that probability and coming face to face with the actual woman were two very different matters.

Hesitating at the door, she saw that Ben and Abby Williams were already in the dining room, talking quietly in front of the glass case that held some of the African artifacts Olaf Larsen had collected on a long-ago trip.

Several others were seated at the table. As Terry watched, Abby laughed at something Ben said, shaking back her light brown hair, and he smiled at her, his liking and admiration plain. For the first time since Terry had seen him again, there was no tension in his face.

God, she thought, I've really lost him. And for the first time she realized just how much she had been hoping their relationship could be salvaged. Wishing she could be invisible, she opened the dining room's glass door and walked in. Immediately Ben glanced her way. With a faint furrowing of his brow, he motioned her to join them.

"I'd like you to meet someone," he said with that superlative control of his. "Abby, this is Terry Daniels, the student I told you about. Terry, Abby Williams. Abby has been photographing my birds."

Terry nodded, keeping her face expressionless except for what she hoped was a friendly smile as she shook Abby's hand. "Arch was telling me about your work," she said. "How do you do, Miss Williams?"

Abby smiled. "It's *Mrs.* Williams, but let's not be formal," she said. "I'm happy to know you. But you realize, Ben, Terry and I met just this morning at the drugstore film counter."

"Is that so?" Ben gave Terry an enigmatic look, then ushered Abby to the table as Ann brought in lunch, leaving Terry to fend for herself.

Seated between Arch and Bob, Terry could not hear much of the almost private conversation that ensued between Ben and Abby at the far end of the table.

She tried not to look at them, but only to concentrate on her franks and baked beans, though she had little appetite. I wonder what he's told her about me, she thought. Probably not very much. I didn't see a flicker of jealousy in her eyes.

Neither Janet nor Dave Thornton had returned, but toward the end of lunch the conversation turned to the panther sighting again. Immediately Abby expressed interest, asking to be brought up to date.

"Just to get one shot of a Florida panther at the station would be one of the highlights of my career," she said finally, glancing back at Ben with undisguised enthusiasm.

"If there ever *was* a panther out here, he's probably long gone," he replied. "But Dave and Janet are still looking for him on the Lake Annie tract. I'll take you out this afternoon if you want."

"I'd like that very much."

"All right, then."

After lunch, Abby loaded her cameras and telephoto lens and other gear into Ben's Jeep. He started to get behind the wheel, then came toward Terry, who was standing on the porch with Arch and Bob.

"Sorry, Terry," he said, in a softer tone than any he'd used to her yet, "but this means we won't be able to discuss your project until tomorrow. Why not go out with the guys here, and see what they're up to this afternoon?"

"Good idea," she said, meeting his eyes with equanimity. "I'll do that."

He nodded and was off, climbing in beside Abby and starting up the Jeep's engine, then making a U-turn around the little island of greenery that screened the station garage.

Terry watched them depart. Probably they have a favorite spot out there to make love, she thought. I hope Janet catches them with her field glasses.

With a start, she realized Arch was saying something to her. He grinned as if he'd been forced to repeat himself. "I told you Ben wasn't so bad," he said.

She didn't reply.

With a grim set to her jaw, Terry accompanied Arch and Bob to the lab to collect their tape recorder and a sack of peanuts. They struck out through a gate behind the station headquarters, then crossed a weathered board that spanned a drainage ditch.

Ahead, beyond the railroad right-of-way, the scrub glistened in the midday sun, the leaves of Chapman's oak and palmetto licked with light. Insect humming rose and fell in an almost musical cadence.

As they walked, Terry's heels sank into the soft, rutted sand, reminding her that her calves would be sore in the morning.

Her sunburn would have deepened too, as well as her pain at being so near Ben, only to have an unbridgeable distance separate them.

I hate him, she thought, as she watched Bob offer peanuts to some of the jays, inviting them with his best imitation of their call. If he's in love with Abby, he didn't have to kiss me like that last night, making me feel all that wild longing again.

"You want to try it?" Bob asked.

"Okay." Taking the peanut he held out to her, she offered it, and forgot her unhappy thoughts for the moment as one of the softly colored blue-and-gray birds swooped down to fasten itself to her hand and peck the nut kernels out of the shell.

"They're really something, aren't they?" said Arch. "A pleasure to work with, as I guess you know."

"Yes," said Terry. "I'm glad to be back," she added, suddenly meaning it. Yet she was quiet as her companions reached the territory they had been studying and began to take notes.

This is the life I've missed. And not just Ben, she thought, as she watched the birds defend against encroachment by neighboring jays. But I want him to be part of it. Maybe I do hate him sometimes, but that's still how it is. Against all reason, she wondered if she had a chance.

It was hot out in the scrub, blisteringly hot for the end of March, and they returned to the station early. Angry with her own confused emotions, Terry found herself hoping to get a moment alone with Ben.

But at supper, someone mentioned that he and Abby had gone into Lake Placid and wouldn't be back until late. She spent a pensive evening with Bob and Arch. Tired, out of sorts, and feeling a bit sunburned, she had little to say as her new colleagues went over the results of the day's research and discussed some angles she might use for a study of her own.

Then, when Bob ambled off to the lounge to watch television, Terry accepted Arch's suggestion to walk back along the fence line by the cottages and listen to the night sounds of the birds.

Preoccupied, she was genuinely surprised when he stopped, took her into his arms and tried to kiss her.

"Please . . . don't," she exclaimed softly, drawing back a little.

"What's wrong?" Arch continued to hold her hand. "Still mourning for your late husband?"

She turned her face away. "Not really. Things hadn't . . . been that way between us for a long time."

"What, then?" His voice was gentle. "Is it the great Dr. Reno?"

"No." Terry realized her denial had been much too quick, too sharp. "Actually, we don't like each other much."

She could feel Arch's shrug in the dark. "I'm not so sure about that," he said. "But it's none of my business. You can't blame a guy for trying. Friends anyway?"

Unable to help liking Arch, she managed a smile. "Friends," she replied, squeezing his hand.

Terry was in bed already when she heard Ben and Abby come up the stairs. Ben said something in those soft, deep, raspy accents of his, but Terry couldn't tell what it was. Abby replied, her voice low and confident.

Then the heavy metal door to the supplementary

39

men's quarters at the end of the hall closed with a thud, cutting off all sound. As bold as ever, Ben had taken Abby to bed right there at the station, with Arch and Bob in the next room and herself only a few feet away.

Desperate, she dug in her case for the bottle of sleeping pills the Moreaus' doctor had prescribed after Philip's death, then thrust it aside. No, she thought. I'll just have to face it.

In the morning, Terry steeled herself for the casual but telltale intimacy that Ben and Abby would exhibit at breakfast. But she didn't have to wait that long to confront Ben.

She was standing under the shower in the old-fashioned bathtub, lathering determinedly and muttering to herself that she didn't care anymore, when she felt his eyes on her.

Never dreaming her privacy would be invaded, she had not taken care to pull the plastic shower curtain completely around her. Now she whirled, unbelieving, to face him.

He was standing in the half-open door, armed with towel and shaving kit, his blue eyes glinting with the same fire and lazy insolence she remembered.

Without haste, his gaze traveled down and then back up her soap-slickened form before meeting her eyes.

"Arch was right," he said in that throaty voice that had always turned her resolve to jelly. "You're still mighty damn decorative. That's quite a nice sunburn, too, on those beautiful thighs."

His hair was tousled still, she noted, from its contact with the pillows he'd shared with Abby.

Somehow, she managed to gather her wits and bunch the shower curtain in front of her. "How

. . . how *dare* you . . . come in here?" she spat at him furiously.

His mouth curved. "The door was open."

"I *shut* it."

He shrugged. "It doesn't close properly. There's a sign. You have to put on the light."

Clutching the shower curtain more closely, she stared at him in consternation. "You might at least look the other way," she sputtered after a moment.

Obligingly, he glanced toward the sink, then raised his brows quizzically. "Hadn't you better get on with your shower so someone else can get a turn?"

"As soon as you leave." Her voice was tinged with sarcasm. "I'm sure Abby won't mind waiting a few minutes for you."

His brows shot up even further. "Abby? But she left for Jensen Beach last night."

"I don't believe it. I heard the two of you on the stairs. . . ."

Terry's voice trailed off as her face was suffused with crimson. She sounded like a jealous fool. How pleased Ben must be, she thought, to know how I lay there and suffered in the dark.

He seemed puzzled instead. "Oh," he said finally. "So you think . . . Well, she did leave, though not before I had time to make love to her."

"Get out!" Terry could feel herself shaking.

He stood there, regarding the area of the sink levelly for a moment. "The fact is," he said, "I didn't—though I don't see how that's any of your business. Now, would you mind finishing your shower so we can have our breakfast and go out in the field? Just the two of us."

A thousand thoughts were competing in her head. "Ben," she whispered. "Get out of here. Please."

"All right." Ben's mouth—that beautiful, sensuous mouth of his—was curving again. "By the way, your shoulders and upper back are sunburned too, and the backs of your legs—though not the part in between."

Her eyes widened. "But how . . . ?"

His faint smile relaxed into a grin. "The mirror," he said, slipping out the door in time to avoid the soap dish she flung at him. "I had a fabulous view."

4

~~~~~~~~~~~~

Standing there, awkwardly grasping the plastic shower curtain as if she were Salome and it her last veil, Terry didn't know whether to laugh or cry.

Both laughter and tears were welling up inside her, threatening to overflow.

But then she thought of something. Hesitantly, she glanced over her shoulder at the bathroom mirror to see what Ben had seen. Despite the moisture from her shower, the mirror had fogged very little. He'd had a full-length view, all right—of sunburned knees held primly together, the white curve of buttocks he'd once delighted in caressing, even, beneath her slightly raised arm, a swell of breast. In short, everything he hadn't seen initially.

With an insolence she remembered all too well, he'd calmly looked her over during their brief, unorthodox conversation. She had an even more infuriating realization: He'd probably heard the water running before opening the door.

Of course he had.

"Oh!" she gasped. "He's . . . *insufferable!*"

Then she remembered what he'd said about the light.

Shutting off the spray, she hopped out of the huge old tub and wrapped herself in a towel. There was no use in taking any more chances. Ben might be all too aware of how she looked in the nude, but Arch and Bob Dawes didn't need to join in the fun.

With the safety signal of the light flicked on, she dried off quickly and tied her robe around her. She fled to her room without encountering anyone.

A moment later, as she vigorously fluffed her short blond curls, she heard what might have been Ben's step in the hall. He had given her barely two minutes. And she could hear the shower go on with her door closed.

What a fool I must have seemed, she thought, reliving her deep embarrassment over the accusation she'd flung at him about spending the night with Abby. *How he must have gloated to think that his conquests could cause me pain.*

Yet reason suggested that his tone had hardly been hostile. And he'd admitted finally that he and Abby had not made love.

As she donned cutoff jeans and a tee shirt, applied sunscreen and a dab of lipstick, she found herself returning again and again to that thought. Meeting her own very sober-looking brown eyes in the mirror, she had to admit the truth. Something in her had leaped at his admission, had rejoiced in the announcement that they would go out into the field together, "just the two of us."

Yes, she had been on the verge of laughing when she'd thrown the soap dish, out of sheer pleasure that her feminine attributes were appreciated, that the two of them might have some kind of relationship beyond enmity again. Most especially because the Ben who was all lusting, teasing male was one she felt best equipped to handle.

Just the same, it will be difficult to stare him down over grits and bacon with all the others at that long table, she thought. I'll be tongue-tied and embarrassed. Or I'll catch his eye and burst out laughing.

He was a few minutes late to breakfast, his dark hair still a bit damp where it curled about his ears. He had chosen a blue work shirt, which set off his tan and made his eyes seem heartbreakingly blue.

Already the day was warm, and he had rolled up his shirt sleeves and left the front partially unbuttoned to expose a slim triangle of dark chest hair. Probably long before noon he would shed the shirt altogether, and she would be hard put to avert her eyes from his broad shoulders and narrow waist, the movement of hard smooth muscles under his bronzed skin.

If this morning were any indication . . . But there was no hint in his manner of what had passed between them in the big old-fashioned bathroom, no inkling of what might be to come.

Characteristically, after his unmerciful teasing upstairs, he now made things easy for her. Nodding to her with a friendly if impersonal "Good morning," he helped himself to eggs and spread marmalade on his toast before turning to Arch and Bob.

"I'd like the two of you to help Dr. Thornton and Janet this morning," he said. "I saw some tracks out at Lake Annie yesterday that might have been made by a panther. Though they weren't fresh and it was difficult to tell, I think Janet may have been right. Of course, that cat could be thirty miles from here by now."

Dave Thornton raised his brows in surprise. The possible authenticity of the panther tracks was not news to him. But Terry guessed he hadn't been told about getting the extra help.

Arch caught the look and shot her an inquiring glance. She shrugged, willing herself not to look down at her plate.

"Naturally, Janet and I will appreciate any assistance," said Dave mildly after a moment. "By the way, where is she this morning?"

"She went out early."

Arch put down his coffee cup. "What about Terry? Is she coming with us?"

Ben shook his head, fixing Terry with his blue gaze. There was just the faintest tug of amusement at the corner of his mouth. "No," he said. "We're going out to discuss her project today."

The friendly malice in Arch's green eyes needed no interpretation. So it is the great Dr. Reno after all, he was telling her.

"Yell if you need me," he whispered on the porch before getting into the Jeep with Dave and Bob. "But don't wait until all is nearly lost. These sand hills might slow me down some in coming to your rescue."

"You're terrible," Terry replied, giving him a little push. "I suppose I'd be safer with you."

"Better off," said Arch. "But that's just one man's opinion."

To Terry's chagrin, Ben had come outside in time to overhear most of their little exchange. Again she saw that slight twitch of muscle alongside his mouth.

"I see you've made a conquest," he commented dryly, as the Jeep with Dave and Arch and Bob disappeared from view. "C'mon. Let's go down to the lab and get some binoculars."

Lightly, briefly, he touched the small of her back with one hand. It was merely a gesture of male politeness, one that indicated she should precede him up the steps.

Yet it sent an electric awareness of him coursing through her, a vivid consciousness of his tall presence behind her. Without turning to look, she could imagine the breadth of his shoulders, the ironic light in those blue eyes, the shape of his hands. She longed suddenly to have those hands touch her again, just to have him rest one casually on her shoulder.

Where is the hostility I felt down by the soft-drink machine? she asked herself. I don't feel it now.

Ben slid the lab door open. "I'll get the binoculars," he said. "Do you want to take some iced tea? There's a canteen on the shelf by the refrigerator."

Quietly she poured tea into the canteen from a container he kept nestled beside specimens and chemicals that required cold storage.

Selecting two pairs of binoculars, Ben slipped a pen and his tiny record-keeping notebook into the back pocket of his shorts. Then he opened a desk drawer and withdrew something that looked like a slim booklet covered in dusty blue.

"Have you seen this?" he asked.

She came over to stand beside him. He was holding out a copy of the first monograph written on the jays, the upshot of the research they'd begun together long ago. Her father was listed as principal investigator. Ben's name appeared below his, and then Terry's: *Theresa M. Daniels.*

"Yes," she said, taking the booklet from his hands. "My father saw to it that I had a copy. He . . . said you were responsible for the printing."

Ben nodded. "I was."

"I've always wondered . . . why you listed my name

like that, even though it had changed by the time this was published."

He did not react to her oblique reference to Philip and her marriage. Instead, he merely regarded her soberly. "You were Theresa Daniels when you worked on the project," he said. "It seemed . . . appropriate that you be listed as your father's daughter."

For a moment, she didn't reply, but only stood there holding the monograph in her hands. If I had been Theresa Reno by the time this was published, I have no doubt that's how my name would have appeared, she thought.

"I'm glad now that you did list it this way," she said, handing it back to him.

Without commenting further, he replaced the booklet in his desk and handed her a pair of binoculars. "Let's go," he said.

Walking out with him into the clear, brilliant sunlight, she resolved not to think of the past but to keep the sensations of the moment, the work they would do that morning, uppermost in her mind. He was whistling faintly under his breath the way she remembered, and she enjoyed the companionable sound of it, just as she enjoyed the sun on her neck, the calls of the birds and insects.

It was hard to believe that she was actually there, accompanying Ben into the field again, after a separation she had thought must last both their lifetimes. Yet this morning, it seemed the most natural thing in the world.

Single file, they crossed the tracks and the drainage ditch. Before them the scrub stretched dry and green, dotted with an occasional pine tree or small hammock, the saw-edged leaves of palmettos glistening in the harsh light.

If I hadn't turned on the TV that day, she thought, I might not be here now. I might never have come back at all. Though at the moment she didn't know where their relationship might go, being near him and doing her work again was enough. She felt light and free, herself once more after six years of living someone else's life.

In the scrub, the hoarsely sibilant calls of the jays greeted them. More softly colored now during the mating season than at any other time of the year, the blue-and-gray birds flitted from branch to branch, ready to defend their territories against possible intruders.

"Did you bring any peanuts?" she asked.

With a little smile, he dug one out of his pocket and handed it to her. Expertly, she whistled an imitation of the jays' call and a moment later one of the more aggressive birds had wrapped its tiny talons around her finger.

"I *do* love them," she said.

"I know," he replied. "You were always a natural. Let me tell you about the work."

Tossing the empty shell aside, she walked beside him along the sandy track as he told her how the birds' territories were remapped each year.

"Some of the breeders disappear or die and new pairs move in," he said. "Or young adults take over part of their parents' claim. It's just like real estate changing hands. I've got complete records in the lab."

"I'd like to see them. What are you working on now?"

"A couple of things. We have to locate all the new nests. I'm out here every day playing psychological games with these birds, trying to get them to lead me to their secret hideaways."

"Maybe I can help."

"I'm counting on it. I'm up to my ears with work at the moment. There's a bird survey for the Fish and Wildlife Service on Sanibel, and a manuscript waiting to claim my leisure hours. . . ."

Except when Abby is here, she rejoined silently, hating herself. "Another book?" she asked.

He gave her a swift glance, as if assessing her opinion of his project with Avery Wilder. "No . . . this will be a monograph. Highest academic standards."

"What's it about?"

"Young adult birds helping at the nest. Why and how they help. . . . The Larsen problem isn't making it any easier for me to finish." He paused. "Has anyone told you about that?"

"No. I've been curious."

"Well, you remember Olaf Larsen's son Victor, don't you?"

She nodded. "A red-faced, blustery man. He didn't really seem to listen much when Pop tried to explain ecology to him."

"That's Victor. He's always resented the fact that his father gave away a piece of the family real estate for the cause of science. Now he's about to get his revenge and he plans to use Lake Annie to do it."

"What's Lake Annie? I don't remember it."

"The parcel was tied up in litigation when we first visited here. It's a nice piece of scrub and bayhead and black gum swamp—about four hundred acres. It has the only known lake on the Southern Coastal Plain with a history of continuous sedimentation since Pleistocene times."

"A hundred million years ago."

"That's right. And he wants to drain and fill it, turn it into waterfront property for low-budget retirees."

She winced. "Can he do that?"

"We have a fifteen-year lease for research and it's up this fall. Larsen is already making plans. He's filed a petition with the county to change the underlying zoning to medium-density residential. But, even if he doesn't get his way, he'll run a herd of cattle in there the day it reverts and it will be irrevocably changed."

Ben stopped to take a breath. "Subdivisions for retirees are okay. But Larsen has plenty of other property to develop, property that isn't fragile or unique. I get pretty damn mad when I think about it." He paused. "Want to stop for a sip of that tea? Biologists' rest station." He indicated a pair of stumps under the shade of a dwarf live oak.

"All right." Slipping the canteen off her shoulder, she handed it to him. After taking a deep draught, he passed it back, giving her that enigmatic, blue-eyed look of his she remembered so well.

"Isn't there anything you can do?" she asked.

"About Larsen? Well, we're going to fight the zoning change, of course. And we're trying one other thing. Along with Dave, I've been lobbying Tallahassee to designate the area a public wilderness and buy it off Larsen when it passes into his hands. That would mean more problems—condemnation proceedings and no end of trouble around here. But it would be worth it."

Ben paused, reaching for the tea again. "I've been wondering something," he said. "Exactly when did you get the idea of coming back down here?"

She was nonplussed. "I . . . would hate to confess that," she said.

His blue eyes glittered at her. "You can tell me," he said. "We're old friends."

The words caught absurdly at her emotions. More

51

than that, she told him silently. A lot more than that. "I saw you on television," she replied. "On the 'Bob Doherty Show.'"

He laughed. "I'll bet Avery Wilder made you mad as hell."

"As a matter of fact, he did. I didn't care for all of your ideas, either. But hearing you talk made me realize again what kind of researcher you are, that there wouldn't be anybody better to guide me now."

Ben was suddenly sober. "Thank you," he said. "I appreciate that . . . more than you can guess. There are those in the scientific community, you know, who don't approve of Wilder, or of me for associating with him. They say I've sold out for notoriety and big bucks."

"I didn't believe that."

He shrugged. "I won't deny that the financial rewards have been satisfying. But the truth is, I just saw a chance to give one of those self-help books a basis in fact. I . . . suppose I'm doing the monograph now to prove to my critics that I'm the serious scientist I've always been."

She appraised him for a moment. "What's your deadline?" she asked.

"April fifteenth. I've got exactly three weeks. I've been invited to present it before the American Ornithological Association's annual meeting, in St. Petersburg Beach. It's a chance I don't want to miss."

Knowing Ben and his stubborn determination when he was faced with an obstacle or challenge, Terry was certain the paper would establish beyond the shadow of a doubt that he was a first-class scientist. His personal vigor and charm would also weigh in his favor, and his unorthodoxy would be forgiven, perhaps even secretly admired.

"Well, good luck," she said with a smile. "You'll

convince them. You always did have a way with words."

"Thanks." Ben reached over to put one finger lightly alongside her mouth. "You ought to smile more often," he said. "It makes that dimple flash in just the way I remember."

Terry felt herself flush a little. She didn't know what to say.

"It's been a rough couple of years for you, hasn't it?" he said, withdrawing his hand. "Not much to smile about with your father dying of cancer. I admired him a great deal . . . and loved him, if you want to know the truth. I felt the loss personally when he died."

"A lot of people did," she said. "But you were closer than most. He always thought of you as a son, even after . . ."

Her face flaming, she broke off and looked away, leaving her unfortunate words to hang painfully in midair. She almost expected him to get up abruptly and suggest that they continue their field investigations at another time.

But he did not. "And I always thought of him as a father," Ben said softly, with no apparent anger. "And a mentor, professionally. What's your mother doing now?"

Terry took a deep breath. "She's . . . out in Arizona. Married to a retired plumbing contractor. I . . . don't like him very much."

He shook his head. "Things change," he said. "You can't stop them. Listen, Terry, I want you to know that I really regret what I said to you the other night."

"Oh," she said, feeling suddenly as if she would cry. "Forget it."

"If you will. I was angry to find you so unchanged, still so beautiful and desirable that I couldn't stop myself from kissing you. I guess old hurts take a long time to heal."

I'm not sure this one ever will, she thought. Without thinking, she took his hands in both her own. "Ben," she began. "if you only knew how sorry I am . . . for what I did to you."

"Don't," he said. "You don't need to feel that way. We both survived it and I hope we can put it aside now and work together. I consider you an asset on the project, and I can't see why we should let what once was stand in the way of that."

It was a practical, reasonable little speech, one that kept her firmly at arm's length. Don't expect us to be lovers again, he was telling her. I may still find you attractive, but I don't want that now. If you play by my rules, we'll get along.

He stood and held out his hand. "Friends?" he asked.

"Friends." She allowed him to pull her up beside him, telling herself she had only imagined that he held her fingers in his a moment longer than necessary.

He might think she was beautiful and desirable, but he had put it academically, as if he were describing some kind of attractive nuisance plant that had to be kept under control.

"Good," he said. "I've got something to show you. There's some rather unusual behavior going on in one of the territories. It might be a jumping-off point for your research."

The unusual behavior turned out to be the possible breaking up of a pair of jays, even though the species usually mated for life. "I'm not certain that's what's happening," Ben said. "We won't know for sure until we watch the situation for a while."

As they hiked to the territory in question, Ben

continued to bring her up to date. "A new female is accepting food from the male and lining a nest with him at this point," he said. "Our conjecture is that the first female is sick. I managed to lure the male back to his former mate with peanuts, and he fed her several times—until the second female came flying aggressively toward them."

A repeat of the experiment produced the same results.

"That's not normal at all," Ben said, shaking his head. "Looks to me like you've got a peg for your research."

They walked back a different way, poking about in the underbrush in search of nests. Then, suddenly, when they rounded a bend in the road, Terry came on a familiar scene.

"Isn't that the pond where . . . ?" she faltered.

"The same." Ben threw her a blue-eyed glance. "Want a closer look?"

Before she could reply, he had taken her hand and was leading her off the path through the tall maiden-cane grass toward a reedy, treeless depression.

They had been lying in this same tall grass six years ago when Ben had asked her to marry him. Just prior to his proposal, they had been observing several young sandhill cranes, recently fledged from a grassy nest at the pond's center.

It had been a particularly beautiful day, with the low mound of the nest set adrift, floating amid reflected summer clouds. She remembered thinking she had never been so happy.

Now, all she could see was a dried-up nest, sitting like an island in the muck. "It's dry," she said in a small voice.

"Boggy," he corrected. "It will start to fill up late next

month or in early May." Then he spotted something
and pulled her down beside him in the grass. "Red-
shouldered hawk," he whispered, lifting his binoculars.
"Did you see him?"

She shook her head.

"Over there . . . in that tall loblolly bay."

She heard the hawk's piercing whistle before she saw
him, soaring out of the bay tree and unfolding what
might have been a forty-inch wingspread against the
blue of the sky.

"Beautiful," she whispered, putting down her binoculars after the hawk had become a mere speck in the
distance. "Being here is like coming alive again."

Ben was very close, the warm, muscular length of
him stretched out beside her in the grass. Along with the
scent of bog and woodland, she could identify the faint
mossy tang she had recognized in the bottle on the
washstand. As near as he was, she could not help
noticing his neatly manicured nails, light against the tan
of his fingers. There were bits of grass on his shirt, and
she could see each of his dark lashes as he lowered
them to regard her through narrowed eyes.

Carefully he disentangled a burr that had caught in
her hair. "I can't seem to help wanting to kiss you,
Terry," he said softly. "Tell me if you don't want me
to."

When she did not protest, he rolled onto his side and
slipped one arm around her. His mouth, so firm and
sensuous, hovered above her own, causing her lips to
part softly, their breath to mingle.

"Being this near to you makes me crazy," he confessed, his voice like a sigh. Then his mouth was on hers
and there was no need for words as he moistly and
bluntly kissed and nuzzled, invaded her mouth with his
tongue.

He had moved fully atop her now, pressing her down into the grass with his weight. Of their own accord, her arms had come around his neck. He seemed to surround her, enfold her, take up her separateness and merge it with his own.

Yet there was a testing quality about his kiss, a passion that was held back at first, then allowed to build slowly, as if its full force were not to be trusted. Still, as he raised his mouth only to lower it again in a series of open little kisses, she could feel his male desire, hard and throbbing against her.

She was suffused with the ache of her own emptiness. "Ben . . ." she managed between kisses, "please . . ."

He lifted his head. "Are you asking me to stop?"

"No," she breathed. "No. I want you . . . to make love to me."

It was as if fire leaped nakedly in his blue, blue eyes. "Do you, my beautiful girl?" he asked, his voice raspy and thick as he slid his hand up her faded tee shirt to touch her breast. "Or should I say 'my beautiful woman' now?"

5

On her skin, his warm fingers caressed and prodded with exquisite tenderness and urgency, sending electrifying messages winging through Terry's body.

With an instinctive resurgence of the abandonment he had taught her once, she sought his mouth again and again with her own, inviting him to take her with lips and tongue and the tangling of her hands in his dark hair, the tilt of her hips pressing against him.

His warmth seemed to surround her, making her long to open to him, to give him everything she had and everything she was. In a moment, surely, they would shed their restricting clothing and their bodies would merge in an expression of the love that, for her at least, had never died.

Just then they heard it—the sound of a Jeep on the fire road, a shout in the distance.

"Damn!" Ben exploded. "It's Arch. What in hell does he want?"

Angrily he got to his feet and brushed off his clothes, hung his binoculars back about his neck. Terry hastily did likewise, aware that she was still breathing hard.

"Here we are," Ben called out when she had tucked her tee shirt back in place. "What's the problem?" To Terry, who knew better, the words sounded effortless, nonchalant.

In a moment, Arch was beside them. "Janet's gotten herself in trouble," he said. "She tracked that panther she's trying to follow over onto Larsen's property. Larsen's foreman is giving it to her at the fence line. When I left, he was threatening to call the sheriff. Dave is not to be found."

Arch paused, glancing at Terry's faint flush. "I didn't interrupt anything, did I?" he asked with his usual insouciant candor.

"No," said Ben casually. "Our hawk had already flown. Well, come on. I suppose we'll have to go on over there."

The three of them piled back into the Jeep, with Terry in the middle and Arch behind the wheel. Ben's arm lay across the back of the seat, behind her shoulders.

I wonder what would have happened if Arch hadn't come when he did, Terry asked herself as her red-headed fellow student turned the Jeep around and they bounced off down the rutted track. But she knew the answer well enough. We'd have been lovers again, the way I wanted, she rejoiced silently, aware of Ben's hard bare thigh against her own softer one. We'd be hidden away in the tall grass, locked in loving communion.

She didn't dare look at him now.

At Lake Annie, a shaken Janet was attempting to

stand her ground with Victor Larsen's armed foreman while Bob Dawes stood helplessly by, his beefy hands hanging at his sides.

"If she thinks she's going to convince that lout of the value of conservation and scientific research, she's got another think coming," Arch whispered to Terry as they got out and followed Ben up to the fence, where the confrontation was taking place.

Immediately, the foreman turned his abusive torrent of words on Ben. To Terry's surprise, Ben said nothing, but only listened quietly, gravely, until the man ran out of steam.

"You're absolutely right, Mr. Cavendish," he said, brushing aside Janet's soft cry of protest and motioning her to silence. "She does *not* have her project director's permission to trespass. I'll see to it that it doesn't happen again."

Taken aback, the foreman spluttered, mouthed a few more obscenities, and then stalked away to holster his shotgun beside the saddle of the roan mare he was riding.

"C'mon," Ben said, taking Janet by the arm. "Let's go before you cause any more trouble. Don't you realize that you're only adding weight to their case? That this kind of thing will be brought up when the zoning question is aired?"

Janet hung her head. She obviously saw Ben's point. "I'm . . . sorry," she said. "I'll try not to do it again. I just couldn't bear it if a panther were shot."

They were a subdued group at lunch, each immersed in his own separate thoughts. For her part, Terry could think of nothing other than the intimate scene that had been enacted earlier at the cranes' pond, carrying out in fantasy its aborted conclusion.

In the company of the others, she found it difficult to

judge whether or not Ben might be similarly occupied. Did he feel regret for the missed opportunity, or simply relief? Terry realized that, at the very least, he must have mixed feelings about her. Had he ever really understood why she'd felt compelled to leave him?

She could feel Arch quietly appraising her.

When the meal was finished, Ben announced that he would need some time alone in the lab that afternoon to work on his monograph. He suggested that Terry and Bob and Arch spend a couple of hours trying to locate nests, and then disperse to their own projects.

"All right," said Terry, willing herself not to add, "See you this evening."

"What is your project?" Arch queried as Ben walked off down the veranda toward the lab, out of earshot. "Did you acquire one this morning?"

She was noncommittal. "Maybe," she said. "It seems there could be a case of divorce in the offing among the jays."

Arch whistled. *"Wow,"* he said. "I'd heard about that. It'll make you a first-rate topic if it pans out. I'm rather surprised the great Dr. Reno didn't keep that one for himself."

Arch's comment caused her to regard Ben's suggestion in a new light, as a gift. She spent several satisfying hours alone later that afternoon in the territory in question, luring the errant male back to his erstwhile mate with varying degrees of success. Tomorrow I'll just observe and see if he goes near her again, she thought.

But though she was enjoying her work, she couldn't keep her mind on the jays for long: Thoughts of what had happened between herself and Ben that morning at the cranes' pond intruded, only to be nudged aside by memories of what had taken place there six years before.

Finally, she gave up working altogether and returned to her room at the station headquarters. There, curled up on her narrow bed with her diary in hand, she relived that long-ago morning when Ben had made love to her beside the pond and then asked her to marry him.

At the time, she had still been Philip's fiancée. But he had been on tour in Europe with his mother for nearly three months that summer and her commitment to him had seemed to exist in another dimension. Body and soul, she had been absorbed in Ben and the lovemaking that had drawn them so close that they seemed to be one person.

"So much has happened that I hardly know where to begin," she had written six years earlier. *"I have been so happy today that I felt I must dissolve with the sheer rapture of it, and so sad and horrified words cannot adequately say what I feel.*

"This morning, after we made love by the cranes' pond, Ben asked me to marry him. I had just said something about wanting the moment to go on forever, and he said that it could if we got married when we went back to Chicago in the fall.

"'It won't be easy being the wife of a graduate student,' he said, so sweetly that I wanted to cry. 'I can't offer you much. But I think we could make it work, if you don't mind riding around in my beat-up Chevrolet and can learn to eat stew and beans.'

"The thought of having him for a lifetime was so overwhelming that I couldn't speak for a moment. Finally, I whispered yes, and then we didn't need to talk at all.

"I'll always remember how happy we were later, walking back out of the scrub and telling Pop, and how

pleased he was that Ben was going to be part of the family.

"None of us gave Philip much thought. Oh, Ben insisted I write to him immediately and break off our engagement, and my father hinted at something of the kind as we went in to lunch. But I said no, that I wanted to wait until I could tell him in person, when he returned in the fall.

"I couldn't know that a telegram would be waiting in the pocket of the station housekeeper's apron, informing me that Philip had been hurt in a train crash near Nice and was permanently paralyzed from the waist down.

"Even now, I can't believe it's true. The last words of the telegram are like a dagger in my heart. 'Philip insists forget him.' I can't possibly do that now. His mother is bringing him back to Chicago for further treatment as soon as he is able to travel. I have to be there, to meet the plane, even though Ben is afraid that, if I do, it will be the end of things between us.

"I don't intend to let that happen. Somehow, I have to tell Philip about Ben and give him back his ring. But I can't do it right away, any more than I can let Ben come with me, be by my side. I owe Philip a certain loyalty, especially now. And I owe him my presence there, for however long it takes to say what must be said."

But she had never told him. Sitting now with her diary in her lap, Terry remembered how she had felt watching Philip get off the plane in a wheelchair pushed by his male nurse. Later, he had raged at her for meeting him at all and hinted that he didn't want to live.

Believing he was serious, she had feared suicide, even as a desperate plan had formed in her mind.

"Philip and I were married this morning, with his

mother and Jerry Hadden, Philip's nurse, as witness-es," she'd recorded in her little journal a few days later. *"I sent separate telegrams informing Ben and my parents as soon as the wedding was over. There won't be any honeymoon."*

Terry turned a page, knowing what she would find. The postcard was still there, marking a place in her life that she would never forget.

It had been waiting in her parents' mailbox the day of her wedding to Philip, when she had returned to collect some of her things. Incongruously, the card depicted a smiling bathing beauty picking gleaming, perfect orang-es from a tree. On the reverse side, Ben had scribbled a silly and sentimental six-word verse.

Slowly she turned the card over and read its message again. *Love me ever, leave me never,* he had penned, as if he had guessed what terrible sacrifice she might make.

This morning, out by the cranes' pond, she had almost believed that they could recapture what they had lost. But I can't blame Ben for being wary, she thought. I hurt him terribly, and he won't find it easy to trust me again.

Terry was subdued at supper. Afterward, everyone went down to the lab to work on the day's reports. She could see that Ben had sheets of numbers, and charts and lined paper covered with his neat, bold handwriting strewn over his desk.

When she completed her own work, he asked her to run some totals and averages for him on the calculator. Finished, she got up and stretched. "I'm going for a cold bottle of soda," she announced.

"I could use one too," put in Arch immediately.

"I'll get it for you," Ben told him. "I need to stretch my legs. What kind do you want?"

In the small half-basement anteroom by the soft-drink machine, Terry was tinglingly aware of Ben's presence. Her fingers fumbled as she inserted her quarter and punched the button for lemon-lime.

"Your turn," she said, stepping out of his way.

He laid one hand on her shoulder. "I'm sorry Arch found us today when he did," he said, characteristically going straight to the point. "I would have given you what you wanted, you know."

She could feel her knees go weak. "Didn't . . . didn't you want it too?"

"You're asking me *that?*" With a kind of swooping motion, his mouth came down on hers just as it had two nights before while they stood crowded together in the small space. This time, though, she did not feel the surge of animosity. Almost carelessly, he'd neglected to reach up and turn out the overhead light. Anyone who chanced to come by would be able to see them.

"Does that answer your question?" he said finally, drawing back to extract his two bottles of soda from the machine.

She stood her ground. "I want to hear you say it," she said stubbornly. "Admit it, the way I did."

He gave her an ironic little smile. "All right, Terry. You win. I wanted more than anything to make love to you."

"Past tense?"

He shrugged. "Past . . . present . . . future. It's one and the same. I suppose I wanted to put my hands on you the moment you walked back into the lab and into my life after all those years. Probably you knew it. Probably you knew this morning I wouldn't be able to stop myself much longer after I saw you standing there like some kind of slim Venus de Milo wrapped in your shower curtain."

"I was thinking of Salome," she said.

A muscle twitched alongside his mouth. "Either will do." With his free hand, he reached across to gently thumb one nipple through her tee shirt. "I want to put my mouth *there*," he added firmly, making a little shiver of longing run through her. "To take back everything I once had. Maybe it's a good thing Arch stopped me."

"But why? When you know I want it too . . ."

"Hush." He raised his finger to her lips. "Someone'll hear. The *why* should be obvious. I'm your major professor, and contrary to what you've undoubtedly been told, I don't make it with my students. Now, let's go upstairs before I fall from grace."

Something in her soared even as she saw the difficulty he had pointed out. At least he wanted her. A day ago she had not even dared to hope for that much.

Almost contentedly, she helped the others finish up in the lab and then went with them to view a sports program that didn't really hold her interest. Alone in her bed later, she hugged the thought of Ben's desire to herself. We'll find a way, she thought. Then, remembering that line from Thomas Wolfe, she added aloud, "What do writers know about not going back to recapture what you've lost?"

She had forgotten how wary Ben might still be of her own motives. And she had forgotten about Abby Williams.

Both thoughts came back to her with force late the following afternoon, a Friday, when she had stopped on her way in from the field to chat with Ann Nesbitt's son, Charlie.

"Where's Ben?" she asked, unthinkingly referring to him by his first name. "I haven't seen him since lunch."

"Dr. Reno?" Charlie asked without much curiosity. "Gone, I guess. I heard him tell Mom he was driving over to Jensen Beach and wouldn't be back until Sunday night. Lots of people clear out of here over the weekend."

Jensen Beach. Where Abby Williams had gone just two days before. Terry realized she must have turned pale under her deepening tan. She felt as if she'd been kicked in the stomach.

How could I have been such a fool? she berated herself, mumbling something to Charlie and running into the station headquarters and up the stairs. Locking her door, she threw herself down on her narrow bed.

He's gone straight to her, she thought. *And she's no student. They can do all the things he told me he wanted us to do together. Maybe he'll close his eyes sometimes, and pretend it's me there in his arms. Or maybe I don't even matter to him that much.*

With that thought, she burst into tears. Simultaneously, there was a knock on the door. "Terry?" someone called. "I saw you come in. Is everything all right?"

It was Arch. He couldn't see her like this. She swallowed. "I'm fine, Arch. Please . . . just leave me alone right now."

There was a long silence, but no retreating footsteps. Then, "I won't ask any embarrassing questions," he said. "I just want to take you in to Lake Placid to the movies tonight. Strictly brotherly love. Okay?"

Still she didn't answer.

"You'd be doing me a favor," he insisted. "A fellow gets lonely on a Friday night."

Half-surprised at herself, she sat up and dried her eyes, though she was certain the ache inside of her was permanent. "Okay," she conceded. "I'd . . . like to go. Just please give me a few minutes to fix my face."

Despite her aching heart, she found Arch good company that evening, and on the Saturday picnic and hike he organized to the ranger station at nearby Red Hill. Partly because of his unspoken sympathy, her self-pity had begun to dissipate by Sunday night, only to be replaced by anger.

What right did Ben have to lead her on, deceive her into thinking he wanted her after her foolish confession of desire? Wanted her, even if only to get her out of his system. It's revenge, she thought, gritting her teeth. Well, he won't get another chance.

As it turned out, he came back late that night and she didn't run into him until Monday morning at breakfast. Returning his "Good morning" with a cool nod, Terry turned her back on him to involve herself in a conversation with Arch.

Ben caught up with her as she and her fellow students were striking out toward the scrub. Quickly he sent the other two on their way with a terse, "Go ahead. I need to talk to Terry for a moment."

"Well?" she said as soon as they were out of hearing. "What do you want?"

"To find out what's the matter with you, for one thing. You all but cut me dead at breakfast."

"So?" She gave an angry little shrug. "You left for the weekend without saying goodbye. What's the difference?"

His eyes narrowed. "I suppose someone told you it was Jensen Beach."

"I suppose someone did. Not that it matters. What you do is none of my business."

"I went to see Abby," he said deliberately. "It's no

secret. *And* to think about things. We were moving much too fast."

"Oh." She winced. "Spare me your turgid thoughts." Her brown eyes were getting dangerously opaque. "That won't be a problem for you in the future," she added. "I guarantee it. Now, if you don't mind, I have work to do!"

For the next three days, she avoided him as much as possible, managing not to be alone with him either in the field or the laboratory. Her anger had given her even more energy than her usual high quota, and she immersed herself in her work, astonishing Arch and Bob with her dedication.

Inevitably, though, she came face to face with Ben in a situation where privacy was not to be avoided. She had gone into the library for some pamphlets late Wednesday afternoon at a time when he was usually occupied in the lab. Rounding one of the stacks, she literally bumped up against him, knocking a book from his hands.

"Excuse me!" Hastily she bent to retrieve the volume. "I . . . didn't know you were here—"

"Or you wouldn't have come in."

Her unspoken assent was as damning as if she'd said it aloud.

"Well, you'll have to get over that nonsense if we're going to work together," he said. "I've been looking for you to tell you to pack your bags."

She felt a sudden chill. "You mean I'm out?" she asked. "Of the doctoral program?"

His mouth curved faintly. "Not unless you know something I don't. I want you to come with me to Sanibel tomorrow, to help with the bird count I'm doing there."

She stared at him. "Not on your life."

"Sorry," he said. "It's a requirement of your studies. Arch and Bob have each gone too. Besides, Dave is coming along. You won't have to be alone with me."

For a moment, she spluttered, unable to frame a reply. "Where . . . where are we staying?" she asked finally. "How long will we be gone?"

He answered the last question first. "Through the weekend. Accommodations are free . . . at my house on the beach. I did permit myself one extravagance from the proceeds of that damn book."

They prepared to leave early Thursday morning with only one minor change in plans. Dave would be taking his own car. His ex-wife, who lived in Fort Myers, was going out of town for the weekend and would allow him to stay over at her place Friday and Saturday to look after his teenaged children. She and Ben would be alone at Ben's house on Sanibel for nearly two days.

"I'll ride with Dave," Terry offered as Ben began to stash her things in the Jeep.

"Nonsense," Ben said. "I want to hear how the divorce thing is progressing. I'd also like you to read the partial draft of my paper and give me your comments."

Dave threw her an encouraging look as he got into his car without her and took off down the drive. There was little she could do. Stoically she discussed her observations of the unusual setup in the territory she was studying. As she spoke, they sped south along Highway 27, to turn southwest at Fisheating Creek along Route 29 to LaBelle.

There were eggs in the new female's nest now, she told Ben. And with the onset of incubation, the male's attention to her had slackened. Meanwhile, the pair bond with his original partner had seemed to strengthen again. He was feeding her without prompting from bystanders.

"Ten to one you'll find a second nest out there when you get back," Ben said with interest. Keeping his eyes on the road, he fished about in his briefcase. "Here's the draft," he added. "I'll keep quiet while you read."

As she scanned his neat pages, she could see that he was doing an elegant job on the monograph. It was well written and beautifully documented—the kind of work her father would have admired.

Ben seemed grateful for the few suggestions she made, and asked her to pencil them in along the margin. As they reached Fort Myers, she discouraged further conversation by turning her head and looking out the window at scenes that were faintly familiar from her earlier trips to Sanibel Island, and yet were terribly changed, built up almost beyond recognition.

"I know," said Ben softly, to the comment she hadn't made aloud. "Places are like people. Sometimes you'd like to put a spell on them so they won't change."

Soon they had passed through the commercial city itself and were driving out lovely, royal-palm-lined MacGregor Boulevard parallel to the Caloosahatchie River. Ahead was the brilliant turquoise of San Carlos Bay and the white-sand-ringed crescent of green that was called Sanibel. The island where they'd first made love.

Almost before she expected it or could prepare herself for its beauty, the approach to the island was before them. They had the windows down, and the breeze off the water with its fresh, salty tang ruffled their hair. Then they were across the causeway, passing over a little hump-shaped drawbridge.

Striated green and turquoise, the clear shallow water of the bay sparkled in the hazy sunshine. Ahead were feathery clumps of Australian pines and twisting coconut palms.

They passed another drawbridge, as narrow and quaint as the first, and they were on the island itself.

She had always loved Sanibel's beautiful woods, the way the trees met like a tunnel over the road. They were a part of her memory of the island. But now there were also huge glass-and-steel condominiums rearing their heads in various places around the island, and slick-looking craft shops. Hamburger joints with skylights had appeared along Periwinkle Way, the island's main thoroughfare.

"Glad to be back?" Ben asked, slowing down the Jeep the way she remembered he always did here for the sake of the wildlife that remained.

"As a matter of fact, I am," she said, forgetting Abby for the moment, and her anger at him. Her mouth curved. "Where's your house?"

"On down past the Island Inn. Almost to the dead end, where there aren't many tourists."

Terry knew the area, but she couldn't avoid a little exclamation of surprise and pleasure when he pulled off the beach road finally, turning down a pine-needle-carpeted track through sunlit woods. At the end, in an open area, was a cypress house, built on stilts, with a steeply pitched and ventilated roof and deep overhangs shading its wide verandas. Beyond was a white strand of beach, and she could hear the hiss and boom of the surf.

"Ben," she exclaimed. "Your house is so beautiful. You designed it yourself, didn't you?"

He nodded, putting one hand on her knee. "I'm

pleased you like it. Actually, it was a pipe dream I came up with once when I . . . was waiting for someone. I never thought I'd have the money to fulfill the dream someday."

"This beach-front property must have cost a fortune."

"More than the book's brought me so far. I'm mortgaged up to the hilt."

"Oh, but it's worth it."

They sat looking at each other, the warmth of what they'd experienced only a few days before by the cranes' pond a gentle brush at the sleeves of memory. But there was the weekend he'd spent with Abby, and besides, Dave's car was already parked in the driveway.

"Come in, see what you think of the inside," he said, taking his hand away.

She wasn't sure what to expect, but the interior of his house fitted her first impression of it as perfectly as she could have wished. A huge bank of floor-to-ceiling windows opened onto a porch over the south-facing beach. The walls and floors were of wood, the latter sparsely covered with oriental rugs so muted and worn she knew he had picked them up secondhand.

There was a fireplace wall of brain-coral rock. Rows of books. Two white Haitian-cotton sofas placed in an L so that whoever might curl up on them could easily view either the fire or the immensity of the Gulf just beyond the windows. She glimpsed a wood and copper kitchen, shipshape, and a master bedroom done in wood tones and soft blues and greens. Its huge bed was covered with some kind of woven throw that might have come from South America. The bed faced southward, toward the tide.

Her lips parted softly as she imagined sleeping there

with Ben as the moon trailed across the water and curtains billowed into the room. His dark head would be on the pillow beside her, one strong arm curving around her as she slept.

No, she warned herself. Such thoughts can only cause you pain. Lest he read them, she looked away, back at the straw peacock chairs in the living room, and a wall of framed wildlife photographs. *Abby's, of course.* A desk neatly stacked with papers and books. Those standbys of a bachelor's establishment, a well-stocked bar and the kind of stereo that looks like an airplane cockpit. A patterned Indian basket full of firewood.

"Very nice," she said.

He shrugged. Perhaps he had expected more. "You needn't just stand there," he said. "I see Dave is stretched out on the porch already with a drink in his hand. Can I get you anything?"

"Would you have a lemonade?"

"If Cassie has fixed up the refrigerator. She's a girl from down the road who's in charge of housekeeping here while I'm away." He paused. "The two spare bedrooms have bunks because I intend to bring student groups out here. Find the one Dave hasn't chosen and put your things away."

They had a swim before lunch and then ate on the wooden deck facing the beach—cold drinks and sandwiches. Finally, at about two, they drove out to Tarpon Bay Marina on the edge of the wildlife refuge, parked, and got into a johnboat that Dave kept moored there.

At Terry's questioning glance, he explained that he had a small yacht anchored in the bay. "I try to get some sailing in on weekends," he added.

The small backwater marina with its bait-and-lunch

store and weathered docks was surprisingly unchanged. So was the refuge itself, stretching away from the shallow inlet toward the deeper waters of Tarpon Bay. There were the mudflats, just as she remembered them, with their jagged, exposed beds of oysters; and the round green shapes of the mangrove keys surrounded by blue water. White ibis feeding. Anhingas drying their wings as they perched on dead branches. The sheen of the open bay in the sunlight.

As she remembered, the variety of birds was incredible—ducks and teals and ospreys; several types of herons; hawks, pelicans and more. She was not surprised when they didn't spot the shy and rare roseate spoonbill. Though spoonbills were present now, Ben said, they would be hidden in isolated, sheltered places in the refuge's interior, away from the marina and the dike road used by tourists.

He had seen a whole flock of spoonbills the year before, he added, at dawn, in a place called Government Pond, which you could reach only by wading through a jungle of underbrush and brackish water. The birds had risen en masse just as he had come upon them, spooked by his or some other presence, a glorious burst of pink and flaming rose as they caught the sun's first brilliant rays.

"That's the cream of this job, the real reward you get for taking all those statistics," he said, indicating the pad and pencil in Terry's lap. "You can't even define what it makes you feel."

She could only nod her head in mute agreement. How did I ever give him up? she thought.

At about six, they called it a day. Ben made their supper—oysters roasted in their shells on an outdoor grill, imported beer and salad—and served it on the deck overlooking the water. By the time they had finished, the sky off to the west was deepening from rose to indigo.

It was a gentle evening, the kind that can soothe, if not heal, a hurt. Looking professorial in the horn-rimmed glasses she'd glimpsed before, Ben sat at his desk, working steadily at the monograph. Dave reclined on one of the sofas, feet up, with the small portable television set before him turned low. Relaxed and sunburned, Terry leafed quietly through Ben's collection of bird albums and other nature books, then went to bed early.

In the breeze-swept bunk bedroom, she slept well, feeling pleasantly warm under the blue woolen blanket Ben had provided. By morning, though, the weather had changed. A cold front was moving through, bringing gray skies and threatening rain. Down at the marina, they needed lightweight parkas in the boat.

As they worked, one thought kept running through her mind: when Dave leaves, we'll be all alone. She felt awkward, a bit self-conscious as they returned him to the dock, where he had left his car.

"Have a good time, Dave," she said, handing his things up.

He grinned back at her. "You too. Don't let them dazzle you at the opening."

"What opening?" she asked over the roar of the outboard as Ben swung away from the dock at low speed and navigated back out into the channel.

"I was going to tell you," he said.

"Tell me what?"

"Abby rents one of the Carletons' cottages down here in the winters. They were friends when she lived here a few years ago. She's having a showing of her work at a local gallery . . . work that will go on display in New York next month. Some shots of the jays are included." He paused. "The opening is tomorrow night."

Terry felt sick all over. What a fool I must have sounded, reluctant to come here with him, she thought. With Abby around, I wasn't in any danger.

"I'm planning to attend and I'd like to take you with me," he was saying. "I hear that your friend Lyn Carleton is down for the weekend. She'll probably be there too."

Still she gave him no answer. I don't want to be alone with him, she thought, not if it has to be like this. I don't want the pain of standing by while he courts his mistress.

"Terry," he said, "Abby is a nice person. If you'd give her half a chance, you might like her very much. I think you've misunderstood our relationship."

Her face flamed. "There's nothing to misunderstand," she said quickly. "I don't think about you and your friends. Can't we just discuss the work we came out here to do?"

But there was no discussion—very little talk of any kind as they worked their way into the outer bay toward Pine Island Sound under a lowering sky.

"I think it's going to rain," Ben said after a while, breaking a lengthy silence. "Want to go back?"

"Not unless you do." She set her jaw.

They had gone a fair distance from the marina when the first big drops began to fall.

"We're really going to get it now," he remarked, turning the boat in a wide arc. "Better pull up your parka hood good and tight."

77

Moments later the rain was upon them, gray and cold, a hard, stinging curtain of water—the Southern equivalent of a blizzard. Almost immediately their vision was reduced to near zero. The maze of channels and islands became an indistinct gray blur.

"Hold on," Ben yelled. "Dave keeps his sailboat moored in one of these inlets, just off the dike road. I think I can find it."

Incredibly, he did. But they were soaked to the skin by the time they came upon the graceful thirty-three-foot sloop rocking gently at anchor. If the dike road was nearby, she couldn't see it. Thunder rolled and rain seemed to crash in buckets from the sky as Ben tied up the boat and helped her onto the sloop's deck. To her surprise, he unlocked the low mahogany cabin door with a key from his own chain.

"I use the boat sometimes when Dave isn't here," he explained in response to the question in her eyes.

She nodded, shivering, unable to speak because her teeth were chattering.

"Terry," he said contritely, as if what had happened had been all his fault. "You're about to get pneumonia. You've got to get out of those wet clothes. Let's see . . . I think Dave keeps some blankets in here. . . ."

One arm around her, he pulled aside the curtain to the sloop's cramped sleeping quarters to reveal a mattress custom fitted to the elongated, semitriangular space, and two dark gray blankets, neatly folded. "Yes," he said. "Here. At least you can be dry and warm."

Did he expect her to shed her clothes in front of him, there in the sloop's tiny galley space? Or to crawl into the sleeping area and try to wriggle out of them?

"You . . . you might at least turn your back," she managed, sounding irritable, like a petulant child.

"Oh. Of course." He did as she requested. With only inches to spare between herself and his broad back, she stripped off her wet garments and wrapped the scratchy, rough blanket around her. She was still cold, and her hair was damp and crushed from the parka hood.

"All right," she said. She longed to crawl into the sleeping area and to huddle there to get warm; or better still, to have him hold her.

He turned, the fire she had seen in his eyes by the cranes' pond leaping again. A muscle twitched alongside his mouth. "You look so incredibly beautiful like that," he said, giving a little shiver of his own. "Go on, darling girl. Lie down and try to get warm." He began to hang up her things.

His words sent another tremor through her, one that had nothing at all to do with cold. He had taken off his jacket and she could see the gooseflesh on his arms. "You'd better wrap up too, Ben," she said softly.

"I will. Go ahead."

Trying to keep the blanket about her, she did as he suggested, passing the other blanket out to him. Raindrops were striking the sloop's fiberglass surfaces and metal fittings like hail. Even so, she could hear him disrobing in the tiny galley space.

Then there was a little silence. "I'm still cold," she said.

Sitting on the edge of the mattress, he regarded her. She caught her lip at the sight of him. He's so beautiful, she thought, like one of the old gods passing as a mortal in that rough garment.

"I'll help you get warm if you'll let me," he said.

She didn't protest, and he lay down beside her, took her in his arms. Still she was shivering.

"Terry," he said simply, holding her close, the strength of his arms surrounding her. "It would be better, darling, if we had both blankets around the two of us. I could hold you next to me. For the heat."

6

You . . . you know . . . what will happen."

He lifted her chin with one hand so that he could look into her eyes. "I know," he said.

She could feel her anger at him give way. There in Dave's boat, hidden in its remote channel, isolated by silver water and curtained by rain, they could make their own private world. Nothing that had happened before or would happen after mattered.

Yielding, she gave a little sigh and shifted her blanket so that it could cover him too. He leaned forward, spread his own atop it and then took her back in his arms.

"Oh, Ben," she whispered. It was like coming home, as if she had never been away, never endured the hell of their separation. His skin was incredibly warm, despite the chilling he too had received. She could feel the dark, coarse hair that curled in an inverted triangle from his chest to his waist. Her head was pillowed in the hollow of his shoulder, where it had so often rested long ago.

"Is that better, darling girl?" he asked.

"Yes," she said.

He reached across to tuck the blankets more securely around them. "Just stay close to me. We've got to get you warm."

Mutely she burrowed against him, letting his comfort drive away the cold. She could feel the steady beating of his heart, his breath soft against her hair as the minutes passed and her shivering began to subside.

My man, she thought, shutting her eyes and letting herself be overwhelmed by the feeling his nearness could bring. He'll always be that, even if we can't really find what we lost. And, then she realized something else, too. She would always love him as much as she did at that moment. Sadness and joy were all mixed up together in what she felt.

A tear must have fallen on her cheek.

"Darling," Ben said softly. "How have I made you cry?"

"You haven't." Her arms twined around him.

"What then, sweetheart?"

"I don't know. Just to hold you again. There's been . . . such a big hurt inside me, from wanting us to be as we are now. Maybe . . . I shouldn't tell you."

He groaned. "Must there always be a wall between us?"

"I don't want there to be." More tears escaped. "I don't know how you feel," she whispered. "Whether you still hate me for what I did. . . ."

"My God, Terry . . . don't you know better than that?" Ben's mouth came down on hers in a hard, almost ferocious kiss. His strong arms crushed her against him. "The last thing I feel is hatred."

"You said . . . it wasn't *love* you felt."

He hesitated, perhaps trying to place the remark. "I'm a damn liar if I said that," he told her roughly. "And a fool for wanting to hurt you. Forgive me."

Keeping the blankets snug about them, he shifted his weight so that his body was pressing down against hers, his mouth inches above her mouth. Aggressively he slung one hard-muscled thigh between her legs.

"Ben," she breathed. "I want you so much."

"You'll have me this time," he muttered. "Never fear. I'm going to make love to you, and then do it again and again, until all the hurt inside both of us goes away."

"Even though I'm your student now?"

"Do you think I really care about that?"

With a little moan, she gave herself over to him, mindless beneath the warm, blunt kisses he was placing on her mouth, her ears, her shoulders. All thought of Abby and any jealousy she'd felt of the elegant photographer had fled. Deep inside her, the secret emptiness of her feminine self was warming, deepening, readying itself to receive him. Passion, captive in her for so long, was blooming again like an exotic flower, there against the background of rain and shadow.

I want all of him, she thought, as his hands strayed to her breasts, possessing them again as his thumbs caressed her nipples into taut readiness for his mouth. I don't want him to leave a part of me untouched.

"Are you warm enough now, darling?" he asked finally.

"Yes," she said. "Oh, yes."

"Then I can pull the blanket back a little and look at you?"

She pulled it back for him herself, baring her body to

his gaze. His eyes gleamed in the shadowy space as he let them wander over her shoulders and breasts, her waist, the gentle curve of her hips, the slim legs she'd kept toned and shapely at a health club all those winters.

"Beautiful," he said. "So beautiful you make me want to cry. You're more of a woman now, sweetheart. I caught only glimpses that morning in the shower, just enough to make my memories haunt me, to send a fire running along my veins that I couldn't quench."

"You're the beautiful one," she said.

He shook his head in rough denial as he put his hands on her to lightly caress with palm and heel and fingertip each curve and hollow on which his eyes had rested. Shivers, not of cold now but of delight, ran through her as he stroked the sensitive skin of her stomach and thighs.

"Still silk and velvet," he murmured, trailing little kisses where his hands had been. "Do you remember what I said I wanted to do, there by the pond?"

She remembered perfectly well. In response, she cupped her breasts for his mouth, then lost herself in tremors of pleasure and deepening desire as his tongue licked their delicate peaks. She gave a soft little cry at the firm, insistent tugging of his mouth.

Tangling her hands in his hair, she drew his head against her. "Ben," she said, his name a throaty whisper. "No one could ever make me feel like you do."

He lifted his head to meet her eyes. "Have many tried?" he asked.

"Not many. I . . . haven't let them. Whereas you . . ."

His reply was muffled against her skin. "There haven't been as many as you might think."

There was no further need for words. It was as if something elemental had changed between them at their mutual confession that they had found no easy substitutes for each other, almost as if a barrier had fallen, one of pride. Touch alone now would suffice. She felt herself come deeper into his embrace, return his seeking kisses with an unreserved seeking of her own.

Wanting only to become part of him, she molded her hands surely to his back and shoulders, grasped the powerful trim muscles of his buttocks so that he was hard and tight against her.

The intimate knowledge of his passion that resulted set her aflame. All too well she knew that neither of them would be able to wait very much longer for what they had both needed so badly and for so long. Her own ache to have him was already out of control.

A moment later he had moved fully into her arms, sought her and found her, plunged within to fill her very core. "Darling," she exclaimed, the word little more than a half-articulated sound as the rockets pent in them threatened to explode in a wave of firebursts.

He barely held himself in check, only slowly trusting himself to movement. His completely, she allowed him to draw her up the ascent to their fulfillment as slowly and exquisitely as he wished.

Finally, though, she had reached the point of no return. Arching away from the mattress, she pressed herself in agonized delight against him, the heat of her desire greater than any she had ever known. A second later, she had dissolved in a profound spasm of pleasure that rocked her from head to toe, seemed to carry her out of herself to become, along with him, a part of the universe.

She could feel a shudder run through him, gooseflesh

prickle his skin as he joined her, the groans that were wrung from him setting off in her another little ripple of pleasure that she couldn't control.

Gradually they quieted, drifting down from the peak in unison, the warm blood still pounding through their veins. The soles of her feet were tingling; a deep ache of satisfaction had settled in her thighs.

"I feel like an ember that floated here, into your arms," she whispered to him finally. "But I never left them, did I? We went all the way up together."

"All the way." His voice was raspy and deep, full of contentment. Rolling onto his side, he gathered her close, arranged the blankets about them again. "It was better this time, wasn't it? Better even than the way it used to be."

"Much better," she said.

Outside, the downpour had settled into a gentle, steady rain. The thunder they had heard earlier rolled again, far off to the southeast.

"Terry?" he said in a whisper, just before they both fell asleep.

"What, darling?" Her voice was a drowsy murmur.

"Stay beside me, sweetheart. Don't go away."

Much later, she awoke in his arms, his breath soft against her cheek. Ben still slept, and for a moment she was lost in amazement at how effortlessly the barriers between them had fallen after all, how right they felt together again.

Yet it was just a beginning, she knew. No words of love had been exchanged, and there was still much that was tentative between them. She wasn't sure what he had meant by calling himself a liar when she had reminded him of his statement that he didn't feel love—not sure at all. For now, though, the fact that he needed and wanted her would be enough. Her need for him was the same. As for herself, she could not deny love and its gentle, pleasurable ache as she lightly traced his brows and the bridge of his nose with one finger.

He stirred, drew her closer in his arms. She remembered the words he had spoken just before they slept, realized what vulnerability they contained.

"How could I?" she whispered aloud, lightly feathering a kiss at the corner of his mouth.

Ben's eyes, still hooded with sleep, came open a little. His mouth curved. "How could you . . . do what?" he growled.

"Go away. Leave you. We're marooned on this ship, you know."

"Boat," he corrected. "We're marooned on a boat." Stretching his tall frame cautiously in the cramped space, he moved back to pin her beneath him again. "And don't send any messages in bottles either, pleading for rescue," he warned. "Because I'm going to make love to you again at least once before I return you to civilization."

It was nearly dinnertime when they struggled back into their still-damp clothes in the sloop's galley, watching each other now with no thought of modesty between them. Terry let her gaze rest appreciatively on his narrow hips as he zipped up sodden jeans, and she thought what pleasure his splendid body could give.

"I want you to take a blanket in the boat to wrap around yourself," he said. "When we get back, I'm going to put you into a warm shower and pour a hot whiskey down you. I don't want you catching cold."

I love you, she wanted to reply. Having you again . . . having you care what happens to me makes me feel like the luckiest woman in the world.

They got several strange looks from the man who ran the marina store when they came back looking like drenched rats, with Terry wrapped in Dave's heavy gray blanket like an Indian.

But Ben didn't seem to mind. He hustled her into the Jeep and drove more quickly than was his habit back to the beach house hidden away in its thicket of coconut palms and Australian pines. The sky over the Gulf still looked ragged and cold.

"Now," he said, opening the door. "You for the shower. I'm going to build a fire and fix your hot drink. Don't forget to leave me some hot water."

Damp, and ready enough to do his bidding, she started for the small bathroom that served the two bunk bedrooms, the one where she had showered and brushed her teeth that morning.

"No," he said. "Mine. We're lovers again, remember?"

Turning, she met the banked fires in his narrowed blue eyes. All-male animal, she thought. And mine, at least for tonight, though even a lifetime wouldn't be enough. "I have to get some clothes," she answered.

"You don't need them. Take a robe out of my closet." The look he gave her was like a kiss.

By the time she had showered, luxuriating in the stream of hot water, and slipped into a deep brown velour robe that had a faint trace of his moss and musk aftershave about it, he had built the fire. Crackling on the rough stone hearth, it sent shadows leaping against the long living room's cypress-paneled walls. He had lit only one lamp and had turned it down low. A Ralph Vaughn Williams piece that she thought she recognized was playing on the stereo.

"*Thomas Tallis?*" she guessed, naming his selection.

Ben nodded. He was still in his jeans, but he had stripped off his jacket and shirt and was bare to the waist. The firelight seemed to trace his aquiline profile, to linger on the muscles of his arms and shoulders.

"One of my favorites," he said. "I've got a quilt for you, there on the couch. And your drink is coming up."

As she curled down under the quilt, he disappeared into the kitchen, returning a moment later with a steaming toddy in a hand-turned pottery mug. "Drink it all, sweetheart," he said, leaning down to kiss her. "I want you all warm and content."

Briefly she tangled her fingers in the thick, wiry hair that curled at the nape of his neck. "Take your own shower, darling," she said.

His mouth curved. "All right. I like it when you tell me what to do."

He had spoken of contentment, and Terry could feel it seeping into her bones as she sipped at the whiskey drink, watched the fire hiss and leap and flare, and drank in the richly emotional, almost baroque chords of the music he had chosen.

Her body felt pampered, satiated. Yet, though she was relaxed and filled with a deep sense of comfort and security, she was conscious of a tingling awareness that she was lying on *Ben's* couch, wrapped in *his* robe and comforter, and that he would return momentarily to set her alight with his touch.

She could hear the shower running as he bathed, and she imagined him soaping and rinsing, getting clean and warm. It was an intimate sound, one he had doubtless noted too when she had been under the spray.

I love everything about him, she thought—those broad, sweet shoulders and slim hips; his capable, pleasure-giving hands; that marauding mouth. His blue eyes, so ironic and humorous. The springy texture of his dark, unruly hair. Just the essential person of him.

I wish I could have his children and live in this house forever, here by the sound of the surf, knowing at any moment when we're not together that he's in the next room, or just outside, or soon to return.

Be his wife, her inner voice prodded. Have again what you were foolish enough to throw away.

The music was bittersweet, with all the poignant insistence of a sunset, reminding her that beauty is transitory. A tiny pang of melancholy nudged at her contentment. When he came out, barefoot and clad only in a batik cotton robe she'd seen hanging in his closet, she held out her arms.

"What is it, sweetheart?" he asked.

"I want you to hold me."

"In a minute. As soon as I fix myself a drink."

He returned from the bar with a Scotch over ice and removed several of the couch's loose pillows, then folded back the quilt so that he could get in beside her. His hair was faintly damp about his ears and he smelled a bit more noticeably of his aftershave scent.

"Now," he said, lightly kissing her neck and rubbing his face in her hair, "why do you want to be comforted?"

She traced the line of his jaw with her fingertip. He's so beautiful, she thought. Will he ever really trust me again—enough to want what we once had?

She couldn't tell him the truth. Instead she shook her head slightly, let her hand stray to his dark hair. "I don't know," she said. "I suppose I'm too happy tonight."

"Ah," he said with a little sigh, taking a sip of his Scotch and settling back with one arm around her. "I know what you mean. But don't let's spoil things. Maybe this time the future will take care of itself."

His words sent her thoughts racing. Does he mean that he hopes we can be together always, the way we once planned? she wondered. At the moment, there could be no telling. She slipped one arm about his middle as if to signal her agreement: they would not let old uncertainties intrude. "Tell me more about your house," she said.

He leaned his head against hers. "There's not much to tell. I had dreamed of owning a place like this for a long time. When the book I did with Avery caught on and made a lot more money than I had any right to expect, suddenly it seemed like my dream was within reach."

"The house must be very new."

"It was finished four months ago. It still smells new to me." He paused. "I suppose you remember the way I used to criticize development on the beach, and probably you wonder how I could justify building this place. But I knew somebody would build on this land if I didn't—somebody who might not care about saving it, the way I do. For as long as I live, at least, turtles and seabirds will be able to nest here without being molested. . . ."

Though he had spoken softly, his tone rang with conviction. She gave him a little squeeze. "That's a beautiful reason to build a house here," she said. "It makes me love this place all the more."

Setting his glass aside, he slipped one hand into the front of her robe. "It means more than you can guess that you like it. Now . . . do you want some supper? Or shall we just make love again?"

As it turned out, Ben grilled a pair of small, tender

steaks and served them before the fire. He prepared a simple salad to accompany the meal. For dessert the housekeeper had left them a Key lime pie, the authentic variety, deliciously sour. And to her surprise, Ben perked some excellent coffee.

"Delicious," said Terry finally when she pushed her plate aside. "I feel pampered and spoiled with such superb food and care."

He gave her a wicked smile. "All part of the male courtship display. Now, if you're warm enough and wouldn't mind reciprocating, I could use some help with the dishes."

The fire, stoked with another log, burned bright and warm as they stood side by side, bathrobed and barefoot before his kitchen sink. Ben washed while she dried and put away, learning as she went where things belonged. If it weren't for my unfamiliarity with his kitchen, she thought, we might be a married couple who've been at this kind of thing for years.

Afterward they returned to the couch by the fire, to talk quietly to the background of some classical guitar and listen to a fresh spattering of rain against the windows. Finally, though, their intermittent kisses seemed to blend into one long mingling, becoming passionate again. "Come on, darling," Ben said, disengaging himself and pulling her to her feet. "I want you in my bed, where we have room to play and move and take each other up to the heights."

To Terry, their love that night was blazing and complete. Body and soul, she was caught up in the rapture of Ben's touch, the mystery of his male being.

Later, as she lay sleepily in his arms, she thought how much the way they were lying together was like the scene she had imagined on her arrival at the beach house. Outside, the rain had stopped again, and Ben had opened one of the sliding glass doors a little to let in some fresh air. Because the night was still cool, he had placed a light comforter over the bed. Just as she had pictured it, the breeze carried in the night sounds as it softly stirred the curtains.

In the morning, he woke her with a tray of coffee on the bedside table. She could see that the sun had burned through the morning haze, causing the Gulf to shimmer and sparkle. Though it was still cool, the promise of returning warmth was in the air. It would be a beautiful day to walk along the beach and just be together.

"Good morning, darling." She pulled him down into her arms.

He brushed her mouth with a warm, open little kiss. "Were you comfortable with me here last night?" he asked.

"Yes," she said. "It was wonderful."

"That's the first time we've slept in anything wider than your little bed at the station," he said with a grin.

It was Saturday. Dave wouldn't return until Sunday afternoon. They walked the beach at her suggestion, clad in shorts and sweatshirts, stopping to pick up shells or note the tracks of birds along the wet, packed sand where the tide had receded, sometimes just strolling with their arms about each other.

With its quiet roar, the surf rolled in, wetting their bare feet and blurring their side-by-side footprints. It seemed right, if rather astonishing, that they were a couple again.

"Do you think we'll argue still?" she asked softly, thinking of the stormy scenes they'd been through since she had returned to Larsen Park.

He shook his head. "Maybe we will. I don't see how we can help it, sweetheart. You're a little stubborn, you

know, and I'm so damned arrogant sometimes. . . ."
Halting, he reached down to kiss her as a wave curled
about their ankles. "But I'm going to enjoy putting
things right every time we do have a difference of
opinion," he said.

At noon, they made love again, this time in the
sunshine on the private deck beyond his bedroom
windows. At last Ben reminded her that they had work
to do. She allowed him to pry her from his hideaway
and out to the johnboat again, so that they could spend
the afternoon working on the bird count.

The phone was ringing when they returned. "If it's
Dave calling to say he'll be back early, tell him that
would be very inconvenient," Terry said, laughing as
she went to open one of the imported beers in the
refrigerator.

But it wasn't Dave. She realized that a minute or so
into the conversation and came to sit on the arm of the
sofa and listen.

"Yes," Ben was saying. "I'm coming. I promised you
I would." There was a pause. "I told her about it," he
added. "I'm not sure. . . ." He held the receiver aside
and gave her a questioning look.

Abby, she guessed, going suddenly cold. "It's about
the gallery opening, isn't it?" she asked.

He nodded. "Will you come with me?"

How can I? she wanted to shout. Somehow I had
forgotten about her. I don't want to share you.

"Will you?" he said again.

For a second, she shut her eyes. Wretchedly she
thought of the wardrobe she'd brought with her. She
hadn't suspected she would be called on to attend an
elegant social occasion. "I'd look a fool in jeans," she
said.

"If that's all that's stopping you . . ."

"No. I don't want to go anyway." Picking up her beer, she turned her back on him and walked out on the deck. The chaise lounge pad they'd lain on at noon was still there, though it no longer bore the imprint of their bodies. Oh, God, she thought. I love him so much and this has been so wonderful. How can he want us to see Abby now . . . want me to stand by and watch while she hangs on his arm?

Despite the happiness she'd known, Terry wished now that she hadn't come to Sanibel at all. I'd rather be at the movies with Arch, she thought, or even sitting out by my territory, taking notes on the movements of the jays. Somewhere . . . *anywhere* . . . where I didn't have to feel.

7

~~~~~~~~~~~~~~~~~~~~~

Ben had put down the phone, and now he came out onto the deck to twine his arms around her from behind. Though she didn't pull away, she didn't lean back either, or relax against him. She knew he could feel her resistance.

His hands covered her breasts through the tee shirt she wore. "Terry," he said. "Come with me."

She shook her head.

"We can find you something to wear. It's like I told you . . . there's a lot you don't understand about Abby and me. We're just friends."

If you knew how much I wanted to believe that, she thought. "Arch implied she was your mistress," she replied in a small voice.

There was a brief silence. "That *was* true," he admitted. "Once. Right after she and her husband split up. Abby was terribly unhappy after she left him. We

96

were . . . exchanging comfort, I suppose. But, since you came back, I haven't . . ."

"You don't owe me any explanations."

"Maybe not. Maybe you haven't allowed me to be in that position yet. But I'm telling you the truth. Since you walked into the lab that day, I haven't wanted anyone else."

She turned and slipped her arms around him. "Then don't go."

"I have to, sweetheart. I made Abby a promise."

Terry's mouth was set in a stubborn line. "Why can't she get another escort? She's beautiful and rich."

"I don't like telling you her business, but another escort won't do, I'm afraid. I'm the only one Mike won't punch out in front of her relatives and friends if he gets looped and comes roaring over there."

"Mike is her husband?"

Ben nodded. "Maybe you've heard of him—Mike Williams the mystery writer. He has a place on Captiva, the next island over."

She said nothing.

"He's a disconcerting kind of guy," Ben added. "Likable but impulsive. Prone to tie one on and then turn up on your doorstep. Despite the fact that Abby and I . . ." He paused, shrugged slightly at his misstep. "You could say he considers me a friend."

Terry didn't want to hear it. She could see that persistence would get her nowhere. For whatever reason, Ben felt a commitment to Abby and he intended to follow through on it. "Then go," she said dully, turning away from him a little. "Do your duty. I don't want to tag along and see her behaving like your mistress. Even if you haven't made love to her for a while."

For a second, she thought he was going to laugh. If he had, things might have been all right between them.

But then he dropped his hands. "At the moment, *you're* my mistress, whether you'll admit that or not," he said tersely as he turned to go back into the house.

The opening was to begin at five-thirty, with a private gathering for a few family members and friends before the public arrived. It was nearly five now. Terry had settled herself obstinately in one corner of the couch with a book by the time Ben emerged from the bedroom. She caught her breath at how handsome he was in his immaculate white shirt, dark tie, precisely tailored dinner jacket and slim black trousers.

He's like some big sleek wild animal in those clothes, she thought, all the sexier and more dangerous for looking so civilized at the moment.

"Sure you won't change your mind?" he asked, adjusting his cuffs and scowling at her a little.

The cuffs gleamed white against the tan of his hands. She noted that he was wearing a different watch, gold and expensively thin against his wrist.

"I'm sure," she said.

He shrugged, a distant look in his dark-fringed eyes. "Suit yourself," he said. "Don't wait up for me."

The door closed. For a moment she felt a surge of panic as she heard the Jeep start up, and she almost ran out to tell him she had changed her mind. But she really *didn't* have anything to wear. And anyway, it was too late. She could hear him pulling away, out of the marl driveway and onto the beach road. Her stubbornness returned, allowing her to save face with herself momentarily.

I refuse to be so grateful to get him back that I'll do anything to keep him, she thought, getting up and walking over to view his collection of Abby's photographs with distaste. He'll just have to choose between the two of us.

In her secret heart, she knew she was falsifying the situation. He had told her the truth about Abby straight out, had made no attempt to hide his involvement. But he'd qualified that revelation with another that should have lessened her anger. Since she had returned, he'd said, he hadn't wanted anyone but her.

In a way, he was only doing what he saw as his duty to a friend. I wouldn't love him the way I do, she thought, if I could push him around. I wouldn't admire him so much.

Guilty and restless, she went to the refrigerator for another beer and then on impulse got her old diary out of her overnight bag, where she had thrust it without being able to say why. With the small leather-bound volume in her lap, she sat in a canvas deck chair facing the descending sun as flocks of gulls wheeled and fed at the waterline. Behind her, the house was quiet and empty of Ben, though everything told mutely of his warmth and intelligence and taste.

He might as well have designed it to please me, she thought. I love it so. I want nothing more than to live here with him, to come back always to this shelter of our love.

Quietly she took a swallow of beer. I want him any way I can have him, she thought. You probably made a big mistake, then, by refusing to go with him tonight, her inner voice prompted. He was yours for the taking once, and you turned away. Now you're too proud to fight for what you want.

With a little groan, she opened the pages of her diary at random. Her glance, as she squinted against the glare, came to rest on an account of how Ben had accosted her so long ago, the morning after they'd first made love.

She didn't need the words to remember how he had drawn her aside brusquely, a little way from the cottage porch, under the trees.

"Do you take anything?" he had demanded. "I forgot to ask."

At her blank-faced stare, he had held both her hands in his as if coaching a slow student. "Birth control," he had told her. An embarrassed conversation had followed—embarrassed on Terry's part at least—in which Ben had impersonally and efficiently extracted the necessary information about her monthly cycle. "Well, we're safe," he'd said. "Probably." And then he'd bundled her into town to see a doctor.

On the way, Terry had been silent, painfully rearranging her romantic notions. "Say something," he had ordered, appearing to concentrate on his driving. "Will this be any easier if I tell you that I love you?"

Her lip had quivered a little as she stared at him. "Do you?" she had asked.

He had glanced at her then, a look of mixed exasperation and uncertainty on his face. "I must be doing something wrong if you haven't guessed."

"Oh, Ben!" They were away from the cottage, out of her parents' sight, and she had thrown her arms around him.

His voice had been raspy in her ear. "So tell me, dammit," he'd insisted, pulling her close.

"Anything."

"Tell me that you love me."

His demand for reassurance echoed now in Terry's mind as she sat there on his porch, watching the tide.

He had been the same just a short time earlier:

insistent about following through on what he believed was right, yet vulnerable under his strength and needful of her cooperation. It was true, she acknowledged ruefully, what he told me about there not being anything between him and Abby now, about wanting me with him.

And you turned him down like a fool, her inner voice reminded.

With a little smash of frustration, she brought her fist down on the railing. At that moment, the doorbell rang. Ben? she wondered. But he would have a key. Probably it was Cassie, the part-time housekeeper. No doubt she had seen the Jeep pull away and was just ringing as a precaution before unlocking the door to clean or bring some laundry by.

Terry opened the door to find herself facing a tall, rangy man in his mid-thirties with a likable face and sun-browned complexion. What might have been squint or laugh lines crinkled at the corners of his hazel eyes, though she couldn't tell which they were because the man wasn't smiling. Like Ben, he was wearing semiformal evening dress. She caught a faint aroma of whiskey on his breath.

"Hello," he said. "Is Ben here? I didn't see the Jeep."

"No, I'm sorry. He's gone for the evening." Something prompted her to add, "Maybe you'll run into him if you're going to Abby Williams's gallery opening. You seem to be dressed for that."

He made a wry little face. "I'm not sure I'm welcome over there," he said in his faint Southern accent.

"Oh." The words slipped out before she could stop them: "You must be Abby's Mike. . . ."

Her embarrassment evoked the beginnings of a smile. "I wish that were true," he said. "And you're

Ben's old flame, the girl he once planned to marry. I heard you were staying here."

Apparently news traveled fast in the small island community. "As a matter of fact, we were engaged for a short time," she acknowledged stiffly. "But that was long ago."

"Hey, don't get mad. When you get mad, the fact that you still love him shows. Lovers who get left out can't afford that."

She almost shut the door in his face. "I don't see how you have any right . . ." she began.

His grin, though it lighted his face attractively, was sad, somehow, and knowing. "Don't you know writers are eccentric boors?" he asked. "Especially writers who drink? By the way, I'd like to make it clear I don't approve of old Ben for not inviting you along. He doesn't know a good thing when he's got it."

"He did invite me," Terry admitted, staying her hand on the door.

"Oh, I see." Mike Williams appeared to consider. "Then why didn't you go, honey?" he asked.

Unwillingly, she felt her mouth curve in a smile. "You're going to say you've heard this one before, but Ben sort of . . . *sprung* this gallery opening on me and I don't have anything to wear. At least, nothing fancier than blue jeans."

"Now, that's a problem." Mike Williams rubbed his jaw. "Is it the only one?"

"It wasn't. But now . . ."

"Now you want to go."

She nodded, liking him.

"What's your name?"

"Terry," she said.

"Well, Terry, maybe we could do each other a favor.

If I fix it so you have something gorgeous to wear, will you be my date? Having you on my arm will make me respectable for the evening. Abby will have to let me in."

He still loves her, she thought. He wasn't kidding about that. In the end, she did let him in.

Mike proposed an absolutely mad scheme. All the dress shops on the island might be closed for the evening, but he had a personal friend who was a boutique owner and he knew where she kept her spare key. They would let themselves in and select a gown and shoes. He would leave his check on the counter with a note.

She giggled. "It's crazy. Completely insane. Anyway, I can't let you do it."

"Sure you can." He gave her an engaging grin and she realized suddenly that his freckles made him look like a small boy. "Wouldn't it be worth the trouble," he added, "just to see their faces?"

Despite all rationality and good judgment, her instincts told her Mike Williams could be trusted. And she wanted very much to go. He was not yet very "looped," as Ben had put it, and maybe if she kept an eye on him . . .

Incredibly, she found herself riding beside Abby's ex-husband in his buff-colored Cadillac and, after a short ride, pulling in beside a small dress shop that occupied a converted island home. A bay window had been added to the front of the house, and in it, on a mannequin . . .

"That's the dress I want," Terry said with certainty.

Mike whistled. "You've got good taste. Let me park this boat of mine where it won't be so visible from the street."

Getting out, he removed a key from the hollow inside of a ceramic pelican sculpture that hung from a nail beside the door.

"After you," he said. "I hope that gown fits, because it's a beauty."

Feeling a bit like a criminal, or perhaps a partner in a zany comedy team, Terry tried on the dress that had caught her eye—a narrow, full-length sheath of crocheted copper silk that left her supple arms bare. The front was slashed to a narrow metallic belt at the waist and the daring neckline partially revealed her softly rounded breasts.

It fit perfectly, making her tan seem to glow. The dress flowed over her body's curves as if she were a Greek goddess. I'm beautiful, she thought. More than anything, she wanted Ben to see her this way.

Taking out her makeup kit, she feathered on heliotrope shadow, darkened her long straight lashes, and brushed her short blond curls until they shone.

"What about shoes?" she asked finally, coming out of the dressing room and pretending not to notice Mike Williams's admiration. "The ones on the mannequin were too small."

"Let's see what we can find."

A moment later he had turned up a pair of low-heeled copper sandals that were only a half size too large. If she fastened the straps tightly enough, they would be all right.

"Give me the tags, so I can write out my check," Abby's ex-husband said as he scribbled a note to his friend on one of the shop's distinctively designed paper bags. "And don't forget, the dress has a matching jacket. You left it behind in the window."

The jacket, like the dress, was of crocheted copper

silk. Embroidered in metallic thread in a starfish pattern, it was just the right weight for an early April evening.

"Beautiful," said Mike as they got back in the car. "If I weren't already in love with a perverse and stubborn woman . . ."

Somehow, Terry had not thought of Abby in those terms. But in any case, she certainly couldn't picture her breaking into a dress shop. Probably she can't deal with his eccentricity, she thought, and he chafes at her restraint. She could suddenly see why Abby would gravitate to Ben, even without his dark good looks and prowess as a lover. He has the same daring, she thought, but it's under masterful control.

The gallery where Abby's work was on display was situated in a converted schoolhouse on Tarpon Bay Road—a quaint building raised off the ground in the old-fashioned Florida way, its clapboards and ginger-bread trim painted a pale yellow. There were quite a few cars, most of them expensive, in the crushed-shell parking lot.

Now that they were actually arriving, Terry could not suppress a qualm or two as she-walked with her impromptu benefactor up the front walk under the fronds of leaning coconut palms.

What could you possibly have been thinking of? she chided herself. Ben may take this as a slap in the face. He may be furious that you are sponsoring that *persona non grata*, Abby's black sheep.

But she couldn't desert Mike Williams now. He had been too charming and kind, a sort of fairy godfather to her Cinderella. Maybe, she thought, if Ben isn't already too involved with Abby, I'll be able to point out the humor in the situation.

She spotted Lyn Carleton first, petite in a pair of

orchid-colored party pajamas, beside someone tall and dark and unprepossessing. The lawyer fiancé, Terry guessed.

"Terry!" Lyn exclaimed, rushing up to hug her. "It's so good to see you." Then her friend raised an eyebrow. "Well, hello, Mike," she responded to his wry grin. "How in the world did the two of you . . . ?"

Terry didn't answer. Instead, she glanced across the crowded gallery as she felt Ben's eyes on her. He was standing next to Abby as she had expected, looking ruthlessly handsome in his evening clothes, with a cocktail glass in his hand.

Beside him, Abby chatted animatedly with a circle of guests. The woman Terry considered her rival was wearing a gray cashmere off-the-shoulder sweater, belted with a wide sash of glacéed black leather, over pleated black silk trousers that were gathered into slim bands at her ankles. With her forties' suede pumps and smooth straight hair, she looked both radically chic and "old money," like a socialite from the pages of *Harper's Bazaar.*

I don't stand a chance, Terry thought miserably. Feeling a tug on her arm, she tore herself away from Ben's smoldering gaze.

"You look gorgeous," Lyn was saying. "Mike's gone to get you both drinks. This is my fiancé, Dan Cater from St. Petersburg. Dan, Terry. Now, however did Mike and you hook up together?"

Terry had the grace to blush. "It's a long story," she said. "I'm not sure I want to tell you here. Why don't we walk around a bit and look at the pictures? I thought that's what gallery openings were for."

Mike returned a moment later with their drinks— whiskey and water, a combination she didn't like very much. They began to drift slowly along the periphery of the room with Lyn and Dan, speaking to people Lyn and Mike seemed to know, and commenting on Abby's work.

Reluctantly, Terry saw the photographs afresh, through Mike's eyes. They were good, she had to admit, very good, each a dramatically stated argument for conservation. The love of nature that had guided the camera was evident in all of them. No doubt Ben knew what he was talking about, she realized. Under other circumstances, I'd probably like Abby Williams very much.

"Ben is staring at you," Lyn whispered as Mike turned aside momentarily to exchange a few words with someone he knew. "What gives with the two of you? I'm dying to know what's going on."

They had moved closer to the circle around Abby, and Terry was all too well aware that Ben's unsmiling interest in her progress toward him had not flagged. But he had taken no step to come to her side. I can hardly believe we slept together last night, she thought. He's acting like we're strangers.

Well, so are you, she reminded herself. With a conscious effort, she returned her attention to her friend. "I'm staying at Ben's house while we do a bird count at Ding Darling," she explained. "Ben wanted me to come to the opening with him, but I hadn't brought anything suitable. Mike . . . arranged for this dress."

Lyn's eyebrows shot up again. "Heaven knows what you mean by *arranged,*" she confided. "Probably he stole it somewhere. I'll tell you one thing. Abby's parents aren't exactly going to welcome him with open arms."

That prediction turned out to be an understatement.

Abby's father, Dr. Davis, managed to greet his former son-in-law with a false but hearty hello as the four of them joined Ben and Abby's group. But Francine Davis, Abby's mother, would only give a frosty nod. The look of bright animation and excitement fled from Abby's face as she herself met Mike's eyes. It was replaced by a look of vulnerable surprise, a haunted and wounded expression.

She recovered quickly. "Hello, Mike," she said, offering her hand with an impersonal smile. "I didn't expect to see you this evening."

"You know how much I've always liked your work."

"Yes," she said. "I do." With only a trace of self-consciousness, Abby drew her hand away. "Let me introduce you. Harry and Diane Goldberg, Frank d'Andrea, this is Mike Williams, the mystery writer. He lives on Captiva. Mike, Harry is my New York agent."

"Any relation?" asked Diane Goldberg unknowingly.

Mike's reply was quiet and immediate. "We used to be married," he said.

Terry, who had been avoiding Ben's eyes, felt his hand fasten on her waist. "What the hell do you think you're doing, bringing Mike Williams here?" he demanded roughly under his breath. "And where did you get that dress?"

"He still loves her, Ben," she whispered back. "And he hasn't really had too much to drink."

"Not yet." His aquiline profile looked stern and forbidding. "You haven't answered my other question."

She threw him a pleading glance. "Don't ask," she said. "You wouldn't believe it anyway."

"Try me," he insisted.

Well, she thought, here goes. People are always gossiping at these affairs anyway. Standing on tiptoe in the low-heeled copper slippers, she whispered into his ear a condensed account of how she had acquired the dress.

His mouth curved downward in a not too successful effort to contain a smile. "You're as crazy as he is, darling," he replied with a little shake of his head. "But you shouldn't have brought Mike. We're going to have our hands full now."

He had called her "darling" again. Displeased or not, he had used the word naturally and easily. And his fingers had given her a little extra squeeze before he'd let her go. She saw Lyn watching them and gave a little shrug. I wonder if Abby knows, she thought. I wonder if she's guessed we're lovers again.

At the moment, all Abby's attention seemed to be on avoiding Mike's eyes and trying to ease him out of the group by ignoring him. She slipped her arm through Ben's several times, chatting brightly. But Terry caught the one or two helpless glances she cast at her parents as if to say, "I didn't invite him. I can't help it if he came."

As the party progressed, Terry began to understand what Ben had meant. Mike stuck to Abby like a leech, gently but with deliberate pathos reminding each newcomer to the group that he and Abby had once been man and wife.

Neither Terry nor Ben was successful in guiding him away to mingle with the other guests again. He kept taking fresh drinks from a tray circulated by the waiter hired for the evening. There was really no way to stop him, short of showing him to the door.

From what little she had seen of Mike Williams, Terry knew instinctively that that would be a mistake. Yet he held his liquor well. Gradually, his Southern accent became more pronounced, though he didn't slur his words very much. The real problem was that with each fresh infusion of alcohol, he became more aggressive with Abby, twice laying a hand possessively on her arm, only to have it shrugged away.

Finally Francine Davis could stomach it no longer. "Lee and I are going back to the house," she told her daughter. "Lyn and Dan will drive us. Come as soon as you decently can, dear . . . and bring Ben, if you like."

As the evildoer who had sponsored Mike Williams's appearance, Terry had hardly expected to be included in Mrs. Davis's invitation. But she had not been prepared for the daggers that were suddenly in the older woman's cold gray eyes. Friend of the Carletons or not, she was considered to be an interloper, she realized— not just someone with the stupidity or bad taste to bring Abby's ex to the party, but someone who posed a real threat to her daughter's well-being.

She wants Ben for Abby, Terry realized with a flash of perception. Not so much for himself—though she must consider him acceptable—but to protect Abby from falling for Mike again.

Abby glanced about her. The gallery was still crowded with people. "It's going to be a while yet," she told her mother. "Ginna may need me to help with a sale."

"Ginna Enright owns the gallery," Ben told Terry. "She and Abby are close friends."

Terry glanced up at him, feeling the connection of their intimacy as a tangible thing even though Abby had her hand on his sleeve. His blue eyes glinted down at her with approval, as if he were thanking her for holding unnecessary jealousy in check.

"I'm glad you came," he said to her in an aside. "And no, I'm not going to the Davises without you. Truth to tell, I'll probably end up taking Mike home."

She was beginning to think he was right. Slowly the crowd thinned, and as it did, Terry noticed that Abby's behavior toward Mike was altering. Though her face still expressed distaste and reluctance, she let her underlying concern for him show through in a way Terry was certain Abby would never have done in front of her parents.

Then, toward the last, Abby excused herself firmly to help Ginna Enright close a major sale and Ben took Mike aside. "You're making a fool of yourself," he said bluntly, putting one arm around Mike's shoulders. "You've had far too much to drink and you know how Abby hates that. Why don't you let Terry and me take you home? No need to leave the field a completely fallen man."

"I have to talk to her, Ben," Mike said stubbornly. "She's been avoiding me. Fix it so we can all go out together for a drink."

"That's the last thing you need."

"I have to talk to her."

Terry remembered what Ben had said about Mike "roaring" when he got this way. He was about to roar now, unless she missed her guess.

Apparently Ben thought so too. "I'll see what I can do," he agreed, "if you'll give me your word as a gentleman that you'll leave quietly with us if she says no."

Mike hesitated, finished the drink in his hand. "All right," he said. "You're a good person and I trust you, even if you *have* slept with her. You've got Terry now."

Throwing Terry a quick glance of commiseration, Ben went off to speak to Abby. Determinedly, Terry grasped Mike's arm. He had been about to help himself to a half-finished whiskey someone had left on a tray beside them.

"No more," she said. "Let me get you some coffee. I think they have some in the next room. . . ."

He shook his head. "I'm okay, honey. Coffee would just make me sick. I . . . need to see Abby, that's all."

Probably to avoid a scene, Abby consented. They were to take Mike out to the Cadillac and wait. She would slip out the back door as soon as she could and join them. She did *not* want to be seen leaving in Mike's company.

At Ben's suggestion, Terry got into the back seat with Mike. After what seemed quite a wait, Abby finally came out and slipped quickly into the front beside Ben. "Let's go," she said.

He started the car. "Where to?"

"I don't care." She thought a moment. "Zenka's, I suppose," she said. "The dinner hour will be almost over. And no one we know is likely to be there."

The beach-front restaurant and bar with its lighted, palm-draped entry would be frequented almost exclusively by tourists at this time of year, Terry guessed. At Zenka's, a three-piece combo was playing. Nobody hailed them as they went in and took a table by the dance floor.

"One drink," said Ben to Mike in a tone that brooked no resistance. "And then we go. I expect you to mind your manners. Come on, Terry. We might as well dance."

Shedding the starfish-embroidered jacket, she placed it on the back of her chair, stood up and went into his arms. Abby wasn't even looking at them. Already she was deep in a *sotto voce* argument with her former mate.

The combo was playing a favorite song of Terry's, and Ben drew her close, putting both arms around her. Resting one hand warmly on her back where it was exposed by the low-cut dress, he let the other slide down lower, to mold her tightly against him.

"I love dancing with you," he whispered. "You're so beautiful and soft and womanly in that dress, I want to eat you alive. It was all I could do to keep my hands off you this evening, even if you do the most infuriating things."

She cuddled nearer in his arms. "Am I forgiven?" she asked.

"You know you are. Do you . . . understand a little, now, why I had to come tonight?"

"Yes," she said. "And I believe what you told me out on the deck this evening."

At the table, Mike and Abby continued deep in discussion, with a little flare-up of tension as Mike ordered a second drink. Ben and Terry danced two more numbers together, in order to leave the erstwhile couple to themselves.

Then Abby signaled that she'd had enough. "Nearly everyone will have left the gallery by now," Ben told Terry before leading her back to the table. "Do you think you can drive the Jeep and take Abby home? The gears aren't much different from those in your MG."

She glanced at Mike, who by this time was visibly drunk, an embarrassment, and in no condition to navigate. "I can drive it," she said.

"Good. I don't want to leave the Cadillac parked there all night. And if Mike is going to get sick, he might as well do it in his own car. You can follow me, and I'll wait by the Carletons' drive while you drop Abby off. I'll need a ride back from Mike's."

She nodded, faintly uncomfortable that Abby would ride with her but unwilling to show him that. In the Jeep, nothing was said for several minutes as they made several turns and then picked up speed along Sanibel-Captiva Road.

Finally Abby broke the silence. "I suppose I ought to be angry with you," she said.

Terry threw her a quick glance and then looked back at the road and the Cadillac's taillights. "Aren't you?" she asked.

The other woman sighed. "Not really," she said. "You couldn't have known. . . . I suppose you're in love with Ben."

Terry winced. "He means everything to me," she said simply.

There was a long pause. "I think he loves you, too," Abby said. "I wish that weren't so, but I think it's true."

Would that I could be as certain, Terry thought. I only know he wants me now, that he's mine for a while. "I don't know if he will ever really trust me again," she confessed, prodded to truth-telling by the other woman's honesty.

Abby shook her head as she rummaged in her evening bag. "He will," she said softly. "I wish he could be as . . . as . . . incandescent for me as he is for you. Or, for that matter, that he could make me feel what poor sodden Mike has."

Clicking her purse shut, Abby lit a cigarette and blew out a cloud of smoke. "Ben and I *like* each other," she added. "Not that he isn't a good lover."

"The fact that you and Ben have . . ." Terry found her voice was shaking. "You're not the first to tell me how it was with the two of you," she said. "Or even the second. It doesn't matter. I want him anyway."

There was a small silence.

"Sorry," said Abby. She laid a conciliatory hand on Terry's arm. "I didn't mean to hurt you. Or perhaps I did . . . I'm so darn unhappy over Mike and jealous of what you and Ben have found together."

8

Terry had to wait a long time for Ben in the driveway to Mike Williams's house. It was an old Florida cottage, framed by trees and raised slightly off the ground, with Bahama shutters, a tin roof and wide verandas. Not fancy enough for Abby's folks, I'll bet, thought Terry with regret, even if Mike *does* make a lot of money. Too eccentric for their taste.

She was still quaking a little inside from the talk with Abby. Though it had thrown her off-balance, the other woman's frankness had cleared things up, at least in that quarter.

Abby was in love with Mike and didn't want to be, partly because he offended her sensibilities, but mostly because her parents didn't approve. She harbored no illusions about her relationship with Ben. And yet, Terry thought, she's dangerous—too intellectually aware of her plight and quite capable of going after Ben at any time if she suddenly determines to put her life back in order.

With someone like Ben, it would be easy for Abby to rationalize liking into love. I'm nobody to her. She doesn't owe me a thing.

Careful, said a voice within. Abby seems like a nice person, and probably she wouldn't interfere if she thought I could make Ben happy.

The question is, she thought, what does *Ben* want? She knew better than to rush things. She'd been back in Florida less than two weeks and they'd spent a total of one night together. If she were in his place, she'd still be wary.

He'd have to prove to me, Terry admitted to herself, that he wouldn't arbitrarily abandon me, or place someone else's welfare before my own.

Finally, he came out and slid behind the wheel. "Sorry, sweetheart," he said. "I had to wait until that idiot went to sleep. He was talking crazy . . . about not wanting to live if Abby wouldn't have him now. And he's using alcohol to drown the pain of losing her."

"I know," said Terry in a small voice. "Philip drank the way Mike is drinking now, you know. He couldn't bear the life he'd been left with after the accident. The drinking finally destroyed him . . . though the doctor officially called it pneumonia."

"Oh God, Terry." His arms went around her, held her tightly against him. "Sweetheart, I didn't know. I'm so sorry."

Her arms were around him too. "At the last, when we both knew he wasn't going to make it, he said he wanted to set me free. That he loved me and wanted me to be happy."

Ben gave a little groan and they held each other for a

moment in silence. "Do you think we can ever put those things behind us?" he asked.

"Maybe," she said. "Maybe if . . ."

"We love each other enough?"

Her reply was a silent one: *Maybe then.*

"I love you," he said. "I was going to tell you that when I got you back into bed tonight. Don't make any promises about the future yet. Just love me back."

"Oh, *Ben.*" Her mouth sought his, claiming it with passionate, open-mouthed little kisses that could leave him little doubt. "Don't you know I'll always love you?"

"Always?" he murmured roughly. "Are you sure?"

In response, her hands slid inside his now unbuttoned dinner jacket and caressed the hard muscles of his back through the fine white shirt. She was kissing his jawline now, the warm skin of his neck, her face buried in his dark, coarse hair.

"Darling," he said. With a deliberate gesture, he took off the starfish jacket and nudged the bodice of her dress slowly from each shoulder until her breasts were bared in the moonlight.

"It's that dress," he confessed thickly. "I've been wanting to do that all evening. But I didn't care for the idea of exposing . . . *what's mine* . . . to anyone else."

With that, his mouth swooped down on her. She took fierce delight in the way he kissed each nipple rigidly erect. *He loves me,* she exulted. There isn't anything else I need to know.

Somewhere a dog barked. Ben raised his head and gave her a wicked look. She could see that his hair was rumpled, his tie unfastened. Doubtless she herself looked a disgrace.

"Here in Mike Williams's driveway?" she asked.

He laughed and shook his head. "I wouldn't mind,

you know, for the novelty of it. But my bed is much more comfortable. And I don't want Dave to come back tomorrow and find us both with permanent curvature of the spine."

Brushing her lips again with his, he straightened and helped her back to a sitting position. "Best put on your jacket again," he added.

They arrived back at the beach house at nearly midnight. "I'm glad you 'waited up' for me after all," Ben said, coming around to open the door for her and lead her up the steps. "You know, it nearly broke me up when you whispered in my ear how you got that dress."

She couldn't help laughing. Perhaps they'd all had a little too much to drink, or else the knowledge that he loved her had gone to her head. "Were you very angry?" she asked.

"Only a little. And I'm going to have to see Mike about paying for it. I can't have him giving you personal gifts." He inserted his key into the lock and opened the door, stepping aside to let her pass. Inside, the mantel clock ticked in the silence; the sliding glass door she had left ajar let in the night air.

"I don't think I've ever stopped loving you, Terry," he said. "But I guess when you told me that crazy story, standing there on tiptoe and looking so guilty and beautiful, I knew I'd have to confess it. There are problems. . . ."

"What problems?" she said.

"Philip's money, for one thing. I don't want to be mixed up in that. And—"

"But I'm not rich, Ben, if that's what's bothering you. There was a small bequest from his grandmother that I'm using now to get through school, but—"

He laid one finger on her mouth. "Hush. Let me

finish. There's also the fact that I'm your major professor, as I pointed out to you before. We can't just go back
to Larsen Park tomorrow and start sharing a room.
People would talk and the deans would hear about it,
not to mention the havoc it would cause among the
station crew. I'd probably be fired. Or at the very least,
your appointment as my assistant would be rescinded. I
want to protect my career—*and* yours—in addition to
having the love we share.''

She turned, saw his eyes gleaming at her in the dark.
"What shall we do?"

"Right now? Go to bed—unless you want some
supper first. I always seem to be asking you that, don't
I? But as I recall, you got only a few salted peanuts and
cheese puffs with your cocktails.''

"I'm not hungry now," she said. "I want you to hold
me.''

In the bedroom, he switched on a soft lamp, then
began stripping off his dinner jacket, shirt and tie. She
stepped out of the copper sandals and took off her own
jacket.

Then she paused, unabashed in her delight at the
way he looked, bare to the waist in the formal trousers
with that inverted triangle of silky, tangled dark hair
running from chest to waist, the muscles of his shoulders and arms gleaming in the lamplight.

"Want some help with your zipper?" he asked.

Mutely she turned her back, thrilled at the way his
mouth followed his hand to place warm little kisses
along her backbone. With some assistance from him,
the beautiful, ill-gotten copper knit fell in a heap to the
floor. She slid off her panty hose, and turned in just her
silk-and-lace bikini panties to face him.

"Now, how about yours?" she said.

119

He nodded. Slowly she unfastened his belt and fly and slid his trousers to the floor. He was wearing nothing beneath them and she put out her hand to touch him, to confirm his mounting male desire.

Ben drew in his breath sharply with delight. "Do you want a shower, darling?" he asked after a moment. "Together, like the first time we made love?"

They stood under the streaming water in each other's arms, making each sudsing a caress, and finally even drying off with the same oversized towel. Then they were in bed together, kissing and touching, their skin silken and powdered and scented.

I'll never get enough of you, she thought, as she arched herself so that he could fill her. She moaned as he moved inside to possess utterly her most secret places. We won't be able to stop this out at the station. Something will have to give.

Later, she slept in his arms, exhausted, spent and happy, dreaming beautiful dreams. He had told her again that he loved her, just before she closed her eyes.

Morning came, and with it the warmest weather of their visit to the island. The cold snap was a thing of the past. In the east, the orange globe of the sun was rapidly rising, while outside their window, the beach was deserted. Sandpipers were running along the waterline; laughing gulls and dowitchers called into the morning air. She saw a pelican sailing on an air current as he hunted for his breakfast.

"I can't think of any better place to wake," she said. He had brought in coffee, grapefruit and toast and they were sitting on the bed eating it together.

"Nor I." He glanced at the clock beside the bed. "Dave won't be back until around eleven," he said.

"You can tell me if you'd rather not, but I was wondering if you'd like a nude swim in the surf before we go."

She gave him a quick look and saw that his blue eyes were hooded and narrowed, the corners of his mouth turned down a little. "Nobody's around," he added. "We can wear robes down to the waterline."

Though she felt suddenly as shy as a schoolgirl, she consented. But she had to push down her hesitation as they went down the steps and the beach path together. Warily, she glanced in all directions before shrugging off the velour robe and running after him into the water.

Warmer than the air, the water was wonderful—clear and salty and buoyant. They struck out, swimming hard, racing almost, testing their muscles to the utmost. Then, laughing and splashing each other, they turned by mutual unspoken consent and did a lazy crawl parallel to the shore.

For Terry, the feeling was primal, as if she had returned with Ben to an earlier time when thought was primitive and motivation simple, a time when there was no delay between desire and fulfillment.

Salt waves caressed her body as he had caressed it, making her feel lithe and whole and content, healed of any hurt she had ever suffered. Glimpsed as it broke the water beside her, his male body was beautiful in motion, like a Michelangelo nude, she thought, but warm, pulsating, alive.

"Oh," she said, rolling over on her back and floating on the surface beside him. "You were right to suggest this. I love it so!"

"I love to look at you," he replied, floating beside her and taking her hand. "Do you know how lovely you are?"

Back in the shallows, he knelt, pulled her down

beside him and took her in his arms. The surface of the water, rolling and swelling gently, was just at their shoulders.

"I can't see you this way and not want to hold you," he said, his hands molding her body to his. Her breasts pressed against the matted wet hair of his chest, her legs against his powerful thighs. When he kissed her, he left the taste of salt in her mouth.

At last Ben mentioned something about Dave coming back and the fact that one or two couples had strolled by on the beach while they had been playing there in the surf. More would be coming soon, to look for shells and take the morning air.

"Is anyone there now?" she asked, glancing over her shoulder.

"Not at the moment," he replied. "Let's go in before somebody catches us."

Wrapped again in their robes, they hugged each other long and hard there on the beach before going up to the house.

Dave was waiting for them in the living room, leafing through the Sunday paper which he must have picked up coming through town.

"Hello," he said. "Guess I got back a little early."

Instantly Terry knew he had been watching them, though he was sitting with his back carefully to the windows. A quick glance at the porch and the coffee cup he'd hastily left behind only confirmed her suspicion.

"Hi, yourself," she said as casually as she could. "I suppose I'd better get dressed. Are we going out to the refuge today, or just heading back to the station?"

"Hold on, Terry." Ben placed one hand firmly on her arm. "You saw us, didn't you?" he asked his friend.

Dave reddened slightly. "All right," he said. "What if

I did? I didn't realize you were . . . not wearing suits until you came out of the water. I didn't stick around and stare."

Ben shook his head. "Hey, that's not why I called you on it," he said. "I want your word this won't get any further than this room. I love Terry and I don't want her reputation ruined at the station. All right?"

"For God's sake." Dave stood up, riffled nervously through the paper and then sat down again. "You don't think I'd say anything, do you?" he asked.

Not knowing whether to feel sophisticated or like a child caught with her hand in the jam jar, Terry excused herself to dress. From the bedroom, she could hear the men talking about whether to go out to the refuge again that morning or just relax awhile and then head back.

"We were rained out Friday afternoon after you left, and . . . uh, we got a late start on Saturday," Ben was saying. Terry rolled her eyes and pulled a tee shirt over her head to avoid looking at her flushed cheeks in the mirror. "We can't even finish what we expected to get done if we *do* go out today," Ben continued. "But we ought to try. Next weekend is Easter, and all the other students will be off somewhere. We can come back and get caught up then."

"I suppose you mean all the other students but Terry."

Ben's response was quietly affirmative. "Naturally, she's coming with me."

There was a little pause. "I'd only be in the way," Dave said.

"No, you wouldn't. You know how things stand, and Terry won't mind. It's your project too."

So they would be coming back next week. She ran her hand lovingly along the edge of his teak dresser and gazed out at the beach below. With that to look forward to, it would be easier to bear the necessary separation at the station.

When finally she came out, with her things gathered up from the two bedrooms in which she'd slept, she learned that they would spend one more day in the refuge and go back late.

At Ding Darling, water and sky and green islands were fused into a serene vista. The heat of the sun on her skin only added to her pleasure. So did the quiet, almost monosyllabic conversation between the three of them. There was only a half hour remaining before they had planned to start back to the marina when she saw what she considered a lucky sign.

"Lookout left!" Ben called softly but urgently, and she turned her binoculars quickly in that direction, while Dave did the same.

A pair of roseate spoonbills feeding in a secluded shallow had been startled by the sound of their engine. Silently they rose up in their characteristically angular flight, necks outstretched and downward-pointing scarlet-and-pink wings flapping, to the shelter of a nearby treetop.

"Oh, lovely," she breathed, focusing in more closely on the exotic birds.

"Did you catch them feeding," Ben asked, "with that pendulum movement of their bills?"

"No. I missed that."

"Never mind. We'll come back in a canoe next weekend."

Later, in the Jeep driving back to Larsen Park through the rapidly falling subtropical dusk, she leaned her head on Ben's shoulder. "They were a good omen, weren't they?" she asked.

He seemed to know exactly what she meant. "I have a feeling you're right," he said.

Happily she shut her eyes, content just to be there, riding along that country highway, with his blue-jean clad thigh touching her leg.

When they reached the station, they moved instinctively apart, not into the hostile posture of only a few days before, but into one better suited to professor and student than to lovers. Still, the very fact that they sat together at all, talking on the steps to the station veranda and munching the cold chicken Ann had left for them in the refrigerator, was enough to get special notice from Arch as he wished them good evening.

They gave each other a look after he had passed.

"Are we that obvious?" said Ben, brushing her hand with his as he reached for the can of soda he had set at their feet.

"I don't know," Terry replied. "I can't really tell, because I feel so close to you now."

Hoping that no one would see them, they kissed good night in the corridor outside her room.

During breakfast the next morning, they said little to each other. Ben was going over some kind of official-looking paper that had come for Dave while they were away. She talked to Arch while she ate her scrambled eggs and grits, attempting to catch up on what was happening with the jays.

He had been keeping a special watch on her territory, he said. What looked like definite nest-building activity had been going on between the male and his original mate, though he hadn't been able to locate her nest.

Meanwhile the male's attentions to the new female, who was incubating the eggs and coaxing him piteously for food, had dropped off dramatically.

"Looks like the other woman's gotten the brush," he said, fixing her with his penetrating green gaze while he forked up the last crumbs from his plate. "I've got a bundle of notes for you. Want to go over them after breakfast?"

"Sure," said Terry. "Thanks."

"How about you, Dr. Reno?"

Ben looked up distractedly from the papers he was going over with Dave. "Sorry, I can't just now," he said. "You two go ahead."

Drinking down the last of their coffee and stacking up their dishes in the kitchen, they went out onto the porch.

"I wonder what all that is about," Terry said.

Arch shrugged. "I have a feeling it has something to do with the zoning on Lake Annie," he said. "The station attorney called for Dave while you all were away. I think the hearing date's been set for the week after Easter."

"That soon? I thought full ownership wasn't supposed to revert to Victor Larsen until fall."

"It isn't. He only filed the petition a couple of weeks ago. Sounds like our rancher friend has been making a few deals under the table."

"Are we geared up to fight this? I don't think Ben and Dave realize—"

"So it's *Ben*, now, is it?" said Arch with a conspiratorial look. "I noticed you were better friends when you came back from Sanibel last night. I must say, you're looking tanned and relaxed."

"You're a gossip," said Terry flatly. "Anyway, it was *Ben* before we left."

"The difference is in the way you say it."

She gave him an exasperated grin. *"All right.* I

like him. We seem to have resolved our old hostilities. Is that okay with you?"

"Why wouldn't it be, as long as I can still take you to the movies?"

Filling a canteen with cold water, they set off for Terry's tract to review their notes while making some field observations. Then they beat about the underbrush for several hours trying to find the original female's nest.

"Ben feels sure it's out here," Terry said. "Maybe if we just back off, the male will lead us to it."

But the jays were being protective and territorial. The only visible nest remained the one guarded by the rejected "other woman."

At noon, lunch turned into a conference. Just as Arch had speculated, the zoning question had become a hot item overnight. The first hearing, by a board of citizen appointees that would make a recommendation to the county commission, would take place the Tuesday after Easter, in just eight days. Though it would not be binding, the citizen board's recommendations were ratified by the county commission in nine-tenths of all cases, Dave said. The first hearing would be a critical one.

All four students would need to free up some time during the week to help with a public opinion campaign, he added. They would need to lobby newspaper editors, county commissioners and zoning board appointees, and pass out leaflets in Lake Placid and in Sebring, the county seat.

It would be a lot of work. Nobody was being asked to cancel Easter vacation, but offers to do so would be gratefully accepted. Terry looked at Ben, keeping her face carefully expressionless. "I know," his direct blue gaze seemed to say before he lowered his eyes to look at his hands. "I wanted us to be at Sanibel, too."

"Offhand, do any of you think you might be able to stay over?" Dave was saying. "If you need time to think about it, that's okay."

"I can stay," responded Janet immediately. "I'll do anything I can to keep Larsen from destroying that land."

"You can count on me too," said Arch. "My folks and I get in a ruckus whenever I go home anyway."

"I'll stay, of course," added Terry quietly.

Bob Dawes hesitated. He was sweating a little. Terry knew he had been planning to go home for a big family reunion in Miami Lakes. "I . . . uh, will have to let you know," he said.

Dave nodded. "That's fine," he said. "I can't tell all of you how much I appreciate your willingness to stick around. I can't promise you much of an Easter dinner, either."

"Yes, you can." The soft assurance came from Ann. She had been sitting quietly at the far end of the table beside Charlie, soberly taking in everything. "I'll be here to cook it," she added, "and do whatever else I can. Maybe you didn't know it, but I'm pretty good at artwork and lettering for fliers. Charlie and I can visit my folks in Arcadia anytime."

Her unselfish offer elicited warm thanks all around. "I've already called Tallahassee," Ben added, "to talk with a friend of mine who's with the Department of Natural Resources. I think we can count on him to come and speak for us at the hearing. Arch, you're good with language, why not sit down this afternoon and see if you can't come up with some wording for the flier Ann's going to make? Try to keep it simple and to the point. These are hometown folks around here, and they hardly know the station *exists* right under their noses, let alone what scientists do. Just hit the conservation theme; make them proud something is being done in their county. Get them out to support it."

"Okay," said Arch. "I'll get started right away."

Ben turned to Dave. "Why don't you and Janet run over to Lake Placid this afternoon and speak to Tom Robles at the paper over there?" he suggested. "Terry and I will talk to Orrin Law at the Sebring *News,* and see if we can run any county commissioners to ground. Bob, you can make out a list of government officials and other opinion makers for us to contact. All right? Churches, too."

Bob Dawes nodded, grateful to have a task to do so that he would not seem to be the only uncooperative one.

"I have to meet with our attorney in Lake Placid this afternoon anyway," Dave said. "That will work out fine with me."

"Okay," said Ben. "Let's get to work."

Ben and Terry got in the Jeep, Ben clasping a handful of pamphlets that described the station and gave statistics on the scientific contributions that had resulted. "We'll have to make an argument for Lake Annie's uniqueness, though," he said, as they took off down the avenue of moss-draped oaks that led out to Larsen Road and the highway. "Just stating the case for the station isn't enough. If my friend from the DNR can convince them the state is really interested in buying the place as a public wilderness, we may stand a fighting chance."

In his book-and-paper-strewn office at the *News,* Orrin Law was sympathetic to their cause. He promised an editorial, to be run in the upcoming Wednesday paper.

"I don't believe Victor Larsen expects you to mount the kind of campaign you're planning," he said, leaning back in his swivel chair and regarding them over the top of his reading glasses. "Heaven knows if it can move the folks around here to turn up at the hearing. I wish you luck."

At the huge 1920s Greek revival courthouse on Commerce Street, they found only one commissioner in his office. Though a citrus grower and developer himself, he promised to give their arguments careful consideration.

They got back into the Jeep. "Think we did any good?" Terry asked.

"Well, we did with the *News*. I don't know about our commissioner friend. He'll have to overcome caste loyalty if he's to throw his influence to our side."

Starting up the engine, Ben headed back to Route 27, then pulled abruptly into the parking lot of a faded stucco motel called the Green Lantern and parked several units away from the office.

Resting his hand on the wheel, he left the motor running. "Tell me no if it would make you feel cheap," he said, looking at her, "but I feel rotten about our weekend getting canceled, and the way I can't touch you or kiss you when I want. I . . . need you like hell at the moment."

Terry thought how much she loved him and how happy she was anywhere that he was. "Go ahead and register," she said. "I'll wait."

9

Walking into the clean but shabby stucco cubicle beside Ben, Terry realized sharply that she'd never shared a motel room with a man before. Whenever she and Philip had traveled together, they had taken a suite, with adjoining bedrooms.

"It's the best I can do at the moment, sweetheart," Ben said, catching her slight hesitation. "Are you sure it will be all right?"

"I'm sure."

He shook his head. "I love you so much.

Leaning down to kiss her, he began unbuttoning his blue chambray work shirt, opening it to reveal dark, curling chest hair. Then his tanned, beautifully manicured fingers were at his belt buckle.

Unable to tear her eyes from him, Terry fumbled with her own tee shirt, then the waistband of her khaki slacks. Moments later they had come home again, in each other's arms, body to body, and the shabbiness of the surroundings didn't matter at all.

Later she would think she had never felt closer to Ben than she had there in the unfamiliar motel room, easing his longing and letting him satisfy the aching desire he could so easily arouse in her.

Their closeness, that of two adults who are lovers but also colleagues with professional respect for each other, had persisted as they lay naked after their lovemaking under a smooth, cool sheet, talking quietly to the silent flickering of a television set with its volume turned off.

Driving back to the station, eating french fries and barbecue sandwiches and drinking cold lemonade from cans, each had little to say. Yet the silence that rested between them was deep and comfortable.

She realized they had stayed longer than they should have. It was already past the supper hour at Larsen Park, and there was a rule that you called in if you couldn't make it, so that extra food need not be prepared only to be wasted.

Somebody is going to remark on our absence, she thought, or ask what took us so long. She supposed Ben was thinking similar thoughts and framing a reply.

It was anybody's guess if they would be able to go on this way, pretending to be just professor and student, snatching weekends away when they could, or stolen moments in roadside motels. But what we feel for each other is too strong, too genuine for that, she thought.

Obviously Ben didn't like the situation any better than she, though she wasn't quite sure how he really wanted things. He had not yet said that the love they had regained might be permanent.

Instead he had told her to let the future take care of itself. Meanwhile, there were problems. He had made one point very clear: he wanted to go on sharing what they had without disrupting either his own career or the one she had resumed. And he did not want to impede her studies.

Terry had been around the academic community all her life, and she realized all too well that marriage to Ben would mean the immediate cancellation of her assistantship as his student. Florida Gulf Coast University would have the same kind of nepotism rules that prevailed everywhere. She would be forced to give up her studies or go elsewhere to pursue them—an intolerable situation.

Meanwhile, if she continued as his lover, she ran the risk of discovery, as well as the prospect of frequently frustrated desire. Retribution, meted out by the dean of Ben's college, might be swift, though she knew such affairs were tolerated in some quarters. Even so, they were injurious to both personal and professional reputations, and she knew Ben wanted neither of their names besmirched. It was a far cry from being two students in love as they had been before.

I'll have to play it by ear, she decided. But I have a feeling this conflict is going to be resolved soon, perhaps as quickly as the zoning question. We won't be able to make it through the year and a half my studies are going to take.

To Terry's surprise, nobody seemed to notice or mind that she and Ben had been gone a long time. That evening and for the next several days, they all immersed themselves in the team effort that had sprung up, telephoning influential people for support and visiting local politicians, distributing the handsome flier Ann and Arch had designed in supermarket parking lots and in front of feed and hardware stores. Ben had even called in to a radio talk show to promote their cause.

Orrin Law's editorial appeared and it was all that

they'd hoped. It urged county residents to turn out en masse to save the Lake Annie tract for future research and acquisition by the state. Ample land for development, less environmentally sensitive, existed in the county—some of it owned by Victor Larsen, the editor said. There was no compelling reason to rezone the land now, but conversely, a compelling reason *not* to.

Also, a reporter from the Lake Placid *Journal* had interviewed Dave, Ben and an apoplectic Victor Larsen to produce a genuinely objective story on the coming meeting. They all hoped the article might be effective in getting out some support.

On Easter morning itself, Ann outdid herself with a sumptuous breakfast of ham, eggs and beaten biscuits, served with her homemade calamondin preserves. They ate early so that they could go out to leaflet the parking lots of churches. The leafleting went on into the afternoon and early evening, when they came back tired and hungry to a roast lamb dinner with all the trimmings.

After dinner Ben had a phone call from Abby. "I'll take it in the lab," he said. "Terry, come along—I need to talk to you about something as soon as I've finished."

Grateful that he had asked her to accompany him, she sat on the edge of the lab table, not liking the way his face grew serious, almost stern, at Abby's first words.

"When did it happen?" he asked finally, when Abby paused to let him speak. "Is he all right? What about you?"

Abby's reply was a lengthy one. Ben compressed his lips as if in disapproval of something that had happened or was being said.

"Well, I guess I don't have to tell you I'm sorry it

came to this," he said. "I feel as if I . . . should have warned you, could have prevented it somehow."

There was another pause. "Terry and I will be down next weekend, after I deliver my paper," he said. "We'll talk some more then. Take care of yourself."

He put down the phone.

What is it? she wanted to ask. Has something happened to Mike? But the look on Ben's face deterred her. She waited mutely for a moment, while he just sat there with his eyes closed, a sad, angry look, almost an exasperated one, on his face.

At last she laid one hand lightly on his muscular thigh, just above the knee.

"Is there anything I can do?" she asked.

He shook his head. "Just be with me for a while," he said, getting up and taking her by the hand. "Somewhere we can be alone."

They walked outside. Though Janet and Arch were coming along the veranda, he led her without a word to the Jeep, not pausing to answer Arch's inquiry about their destination.

Nor did he speak to her as he drove out Larsen Road, crossed the highway and headed up the steep, bumpy track to the fire tower at Red Hill. He pulled her close against him as if for comfort.

It was a beautiful evening, soft and mild; the sky was filling with stars. Insects chirped in a steady chorus and she heard again the call of the chuck-will's-widow, gently plaintive. She thought of her first night at the station, when she'd heard the same call as she stood burning with anger and tears.

"It's Mike, isn't it?" she asked, gripped by a sudden fear. The genial face of Abby's ex-husband floated before her.

"Yes," said Ben shortly. "He was in a serious car accident."

"*Oh, my God.*" To Terry, the thought of it was a sharp pain in her midsection. She felt the tears sliding down her face.

"I didn't want to tell you," Ben said, brushing his lips against her hair. "It was the drinking, of course. They're not sure yet about the extent of his injuries."

They came out at the top of Red Hill, beside the foot of the tall metal fire tower and the garage where the Forest Service fire-fighting equipment was kept. The ranger on duty was just locking the garage preparatory to mounting the steep metal steps to his aerie again.

"Hello, Ben," he said, pausing to give Terry a leisurely look. "Fine evening. I plan to go to the zoning hearing Tuesday if I don't have to work."

"Thanks," said Ben. "I'd appreciate it."

"I don't suppose you came up here to visit me."

Ben grinned, though Terry could see that the sadness did not leave his eyes. "You're right there, George," he conceded. "I'm looking for a spot to do a little necking with my girl. Mind if we sit awhile on the deck of that unfinished cabin, take the night air?"

George chuckled. "Won't bother me any," he said. "Just don't light any matches."

Ben parked the Jeep and turned off the ignition. "C'mon," he said to her, picking up an army blanket he kept rolled up behind the seat.

Hand in hand they walked down the hill a short distance to a partially completed wooden cabin that the Forest Service was building to keep a permanent ranger in residence on the property. Though the cabin was small, it had a wide flat deck built out over a hillside that was unusually precipitous for Florida.

"If it weren't for all these trees," Ben said, "we could

probably see some of the lights off to the east, in the flat area beyond the edge of the Lake Wales escarpment."

He was filling in for her, she knew, giving her time to compose herself as he spread out the blanket. "All right, sweetheart," he said. "The deck is pretty hard, but you can use my arm for a pillow. Let's just lie back here awhile and look at the stars."

She stretched out beside him, catching his faint moss and musk aroma as she laid her head in the curve of his shoulder. Overhead, the stars were like firepoints, but cold, light years away.

"Tell me what happened," she said finally.

"Sure you want to know?"

She nodded without speaking, and he must have felt the motion of her assent there in the gathering dark. "He stayed stinking drunk all week and then called Abby. He was on his way to see her when it happened. He drove head on into a tree."

Terry gave a little gasp, but smothered it against him.

"When he didn't show up Abby called the police, and went out looking for him herself. His Cadillac was wrapped around a big old Australian pine, but Mike was still alive. They've flown him to the hospital in Cape Coral."

She was silent a moment. "He's an alcoholic, isn't he?"

"I don't know. If not, he's doing a pretty fine imitation of one. Trouble is, I *like* the guy, really like him. It's a damn shame he and Abby couldn't be happy together."

"She still loves him," Terry said. "I guess I told you that before."

He nodded. "I've always thought so too. She's a fine person, you know. I admire her very much—even if I think what happened between them is partly her fault.

137

Her folks don't approve of him. Never did, even before he started drinking this way. She wasn't strong enough to stand up to them, come all the way over to his side."

"I'm so sorry for her," she whispered, moving closer in his arms.

"It reminds you of Philip," he hazarded softly. "Doesn't it?"

She nodded. "He felt the same kind of desperation, and his drinking was equally self-destructive."

"You really cared about him, didn't you?" Only the faintest of tremors in his voice gave him away.

"Yes. Yes, I did, though I never loved him as I love you." She paused. "This can't be easy for you to hear. . . ."

Ben shook his head. "I've never hated him," he said, "and I'd have absolutely no reason to do so now. He's dead and I'm alive. I have you."

She felt a sob rise. "And you're grateful," she jabbed.

"Yes, dammit. Yes I am. I *love* you, and those years we were apart were like a wasteland as far as I'm concerned."

Anger had risen in his voice, and she put her arms fully around him. "Don't," she said, filled with remorse. "It was like that for me too. But you see, that night when he . . . knew he wasn't going to make it, Philip told me to go and find what I had lost."

Ben swore softly. "Did he mention my name?"

"No. I'm not sure he knew it. But I'm certain he knew there was always someone in my heart. . . ."

It was Ben's turn to crush her to him for a moment. "Were you happy with him?" he asked finally. "Even a little? On my better days, I used to hope you would be—if I couldn't have you."

"In a way, I suppose I was, though the drinking made

things difficult. We were friends, really, and there were times when it wasn't so bad, when we enjoyed things together—music, art, related pleasures. We used to cheat one another at cards. He wasn't all fluff, despite his wealth."

"He must have loved you very much."

A deep sigh escaped her. "Yes," she said. "I think so. Perhaps more than he would have if the accident had never happened. That's why I wish I'd had the courage to leave him. I think now he might have taken that as a compliment. . . ."

To her horror, she began to cry in great, wracking sobs that seemed to make no sound, spilling out all the grief and anguish she'd felt at Philip's death.

"Darling," Ben urged. *"Don't."* He was smoothing her hair. "My sweet girl, you're not to blame. Philip drank to blur the edges of what had happened to him. You were one of his assets."

With a little tremor, she curled against him, letting the comfort of his presence surround her. "Maybe," she echoed, allowing his viewpoint to sift into her consciousness. "You could be right."

"I am," he said with quiet certainty. "You know, I felt as if you'd ripped out my heart when you left me, but deep inside I think I always understood why you had to do what you did. Marrying Philip took incredible strength, darling. Don't look back with regret now."

"Oh, Ben," she whispered, holding him as though she would never let him go. "Thank you."

The next day, a Monday, she found the original female jay's nest on her study tract. Now she had clear proof that no divorce existed, but rather a case of bigamy, an anomaly that would be the perfect peg for her study on pair bonding. Ben was excited too, when she came in after a day of observation to tell him about it.

They had done all they could do to prepare for the zoning battle on the following day, and now the members of their work force had temporarily disbanded to follow neglected pursuits.

For his part, Ben had returned to the lab to finish the paper he would give that Thursday at the ornithological convention in St. Petersburg Beach. "I should be done sometime Wednesday," he said. "I would have finished sooner if this zoning thing hadn't erupted. Or if you didn't take up so much of my thoughts."

Alone with him in the lab, she leaned down and kissed him warmly, taking pleasure in the way he forced her mouth to yield even more deeply with his tongue. "I love you," she said. "I can't wait until the weekend."

He gave her a narrow, blue-eyed look. "Neither can I. We'll stay over Thursday night at the hotel, drive down to Sanibel Friday morning. You'd better get some rest in the meantime, my love."

She was about to kiss him again when the phone rang. Not Abby again, she thought. It wasn't. "Long distance, from Tampa," Ben said, covering the receiver. "It's about a student."

"So?" She meshed her fingers in his hair.

"I'd appreciate it if you'd step out, sweetheart. And close the door."

Feeling slightly foolish, she did as he asked. Their love had brought them so close that she forgot, sometimes, what his position was. I wonder if the call is about Arch, she thought. Or it could be Bob, I suppose. Not me, I hope. Maybe we're getting somebody new.

But she didn't think it significant. The following evening, they all drove up to Sebring together. Ben and

Terry and Arch piled into the Jeep, while Dave took Janet and Ann.

Terry felt her excitement mount as they parked on a side street, then crossed the perfectly manicured court-house lawn under huge old oaks and palms and magnolias, and ran up the wide steps. She caught a whiff of something sweet, gardenias perhaps, or jas-mine, as they went in the door.

Quite a few people, some of them dressed like attorneys but most looking like citrus farmers or ranch-ers or retirees, were milling around in the snack bar area under the soaring stuccoed dome.

"I have a feeling the agenda's going to be a lengthy one," Ben remarked, glancing around him. "Dave, do you know where we're supposed to go?"

"Hang a right and take the stairway at the far end up one flight." Dave added that the station attorney, John Neville, would meet them there, in the commission chamber.

To Terry's surprise, the crowd downstairs was nothing compared to the number of people who were already occupying theater-style seats in the spacious meeting chamber. A few of them smiled and nodded to Ben or Dave, one middle-aged man giving them an A-OK sign and adding, "You're going to win this thing."

Well, we got out *some* support, Terry thought, look-ing about to see if she recognized anyone. At the press table in front was the reporter from the Lake Placid *Journal* who had interviewed Ben and Dave, along with another reporter she didn't know. Behind them, in the front row, sat Orrin Law of the Sebring *News*. Catching her eye, he gave her a little salute. So he had come out in person. Perhaps his presence would lend them some weight.

Then, startled, she realized she knew at least one

other person in the audience: Victor Larsen. He was stockier than she remembered, his face redder and he had lost a good bit of his sandy hair in the six years since she'd last seen him arguing with her father.

Seated on the left side of the room, he was huddled in conference with a pudgy, rather unpleasant-looking attorney in a dark blue pinstripe suit. As if he sensed their arrival, he turned and glanced over his shoulder to give them a look of such deep enmity it made her shiver a little. With Larsen and his attorney was the man Ben had called Mr. Cavendish when he had mediated between him and Janet in the argument at the fence line.

Arch nudged her, handed her a copy of the agenda that he'd picked up off one of the seats in the back row. She took it, scanning the page to find their item: *"Lake Annie tract, Victor Larsen of Larsen Properties, Inc., request A-1 to R-3, 400 acres MOL."* It was halfway down the page.

Ben had put on his professorial spectacles to read a copy of his own. He frowned. "We're going to have a considerable wait," he said.

Then John Neville found them and they all took seats on the right side of the room, directly across from where Larsen was seated. Minutes later, the appointed planning and zoning officials had filed in to take their seats. One of their number gave an invocation and the audience was asked to rise and pledge allegiance to the flag. The wall clock, placed between tall windows covered by venetian blinds, said eleven minutes past seven.

At nine o'clock the zoning board chairman announced a brief recess. His panel had already heard more than a half dozen cases, several of them without opposition. Two of them, however, had been lengthy and hard-fought, one involving a junkyard said to be an eyesore, and the other, riparian rights in a lakefront subdivision. The Lake Annie case would be called second after the break.

"Want coffee or something to drink?" Ben asked quietly. "I could stand to stretch my legs."

"So could I," Terry replied. "All this waiting takes the edge off things."

Except for Dave and John Neville, their whole group went down together. They crowded in with a throng of others to the little lunch counter with its steaming coffeepots, and racks of corn chips, pork rinds and peanuts.

They had a tense moment when Larsen's foreman, Cavendish, jostled Janet in the crowd, and made some kind of obscene remark to her under his breath. She looked as if she were about to cry, and Ben hustled her away, then bought coffee for everyone.

Taking their cups back upstairs, they stood outside the meeting chamber in the echoing marble hall, elbow to elbow in the considerable throng of people remaining. Suddenly Ben made his way through the crowd to shake the hand of a dark, thin man.

"Glad you could make it, Curt," he said. "Curt MacKenzie, this is Terry Daniels, one of my students. Arch VanMeter, Janet Vickery, also students. Ann Nesbitt, who takes care of us all out at the station. Folks, Curt is my friend from the DNR. I had about given up on him."

"Sorry to be late," his friend said. "I got hung up in Lake Wales on the way down with a problem similar to this one. Glad to meet you all."

"C'mon, let's go back in," Arch urged, glancing through the double doorway. "They're taking their seats again. It's about to be our turn."

The remaining item ahead of theirs on the agenda, a simple variance that went uncontested, was dispatched with amazing speed. "Here we go," Ben whispered to Terry, squeezing her hand even though the others might see. "Wish us luck."

They sat quietly as the county planning director called out Larsen's proposal, briefly described the property in question, and recommended for approval.

"I knew he had a friend in the planning department," Arch whispered.

"Not necessarily," said Ben. "Maybe Larsen just pushed and they didn't realize how sensitive the Lake Annie tract is. It's our job to convince them of that."

"Who's going to speak on behalf of the petitioner?" the chairman was asking.

"I am." The attorney Terry had seen earlier walked to the podium and identified himself. He had greasy hair that was thinning in the back and a defensive slouch to his shoulders.

In an almost uninterested fashion, as if the matter were so cut-and-dried it was scarcely worth arguing, he stated his client's case: Larsen had patiently waited out the period specified in his father's will, allowing the biological station use of the Lake Annie tract. That period would soon come to a close and he now wished to develop the property, as was his right.

He was petitioning at this time so that plans for development could be laid in advance of the date on which the property reverted. The change being request- ed was nothing out of the ordinary. Furthermore, the subdivision, to surround the property's central lake, would generate taxes for the county.

The lawyer stepped aside, turning to glance in their general direction with a bored look. "Is there any opposition?" the chairman inquired.

John Neville stood and walked up to share the podium. "Yes, there is, Mr. Chairman," he said, also giving his name and that of his client. Like Larsen's lawyer, he proposed a basic argument. Certainly it was common to rezone agricultural land for housing. But, contrary to what Larsen's attorney had stated, development of this particular parcel would be a detriment to the county, not an asset because it would destroy forever an environment unique in all of Florida.

Citing what Ben had told him about the lake being the only one in the Southern Coastal Plain with a one-hundred-million-year history of continuous sedimentation, he listed the rare and endangered species of plants and animals that flourished on its shores.

"A panther, one of our most beautiful and rapidly disappearing animals, has been sighted on the property," he said. "I'm not asking you to save Lake Annie for the sake of the scientists at Larsen Park, despite the fine work they're doing there. I'm asking you to save it for the people of Highlands County and the State of Florida."

The chairman gave him a thoughtful look. "What difference would it make to stop the rezoning of the property if your client's opponent will inherit it anyway in the fall? I take it he does not wish to sell."

"No, he does not, Mr. Chairman," Larsen's attorney interposed quickly.

"Well, then?" said the chairman to Neville.

"Agricultural use would be more compatible with the wilderness character of the station," Neville replied. "But we expect that the state will soon move to acquire the land and place it in the public trust. We have a representative of the state Department of Natural Resources with us here this evening. . . ."

In a low-key but reassuring manner, Ben's friend

from Tallahassee painted an encouraging picture of Lake Annie's chances of being acquired by the state. "I expect it to be included in a bill that will be introduced by Senator Burton Francis of Lake Wales later this month," he said. "I believe its chances for receiving funding from the legislature are good."

Curt MacKenzie sat down. The chairman called for commentary from the audience. To Terry's surprise, several persons who had come out for the meeting spoke up on Lake Annie's behalf.

"I'm real impressed with the way those college kids out there came around to my church last Sunday distributin' leaflets to save their project," one elderly man said. "If you ask me, that's American democracy in action. If more kids was like them, this country wouldn't be in the fix it's in today. I say let'em have one little piece of nature undisturbed in this county."

Victor Larsen glared as the man's remarks drew a small round of applause. Terry saw John Neville glance at Dave and Ben, his raised eyebrow questioning whether they still wanted to speak. Wisely, she thought, Ben shook his head. It would be better to let the area residents count this as their own victory—if, indeed, victory was to be theirs.

Fascinated, she watched as the board members discussed the project among themselves, several of them arguing Larsen's side. Finally they heard concluding remarks from each attorney. Democracy in action, she thought. I've never seen it before. But she was nervous too. The outcome mattered so much. Fingers interlocked, she pressed her palms tightly together as the chairman prepared to take a vote.

He started with the board member seated furthest to the left. To their dismay, the first two votes favored granting Larsen's request.

"Those were lost anyway," Ben whispered. "I still think we've got a fighting chance."

The next three votes were nays. Two members were absent that evening, and they needed a total of four votes to win denial. But the board member seated furthest to the right voted aye. Now Larsen was even with them again.

There was a long pause as the chairman eyed Larsen and then looked at them. "Chairman votes nay," he said tersely. "Recommendation for denial. Next order of business."

It had all happened so quickly in the end. Terry felt dazed. "We won, didn't we?" she said to Ben as they all crowded out into the hallway together.

"You bet your life we did, sweetheart!" Jubilant, he swept her into his arms and gave her a resounding kiss, momentarily unmindful of who might see and wonder.

10

I'd like one of those too, if you don't mind," Arch said. Then they were all laughing. Ben gave her a rueful little look as Arch kissed her on the cheek. He clapped Dave on the shoulder, and shook hands with John Neville and his Tallahassee friend.

"Looks like you're all set," Neville said with a grin. "The commission will have to give its stamp of approval in two weeks, and Larsen will keep on trying to fight it, of course. But it's pretty much a foregone conclusion now."

"I'll keep you posted on the progress of our bill," MacKenzie added. "I may want you both to come up for a day or two when it goes into hearings."

Dave nodded. "Let us know as soon as you have any word."

"Why not come out and have a drink with us?" Ben included both Neville and MacKenzie in the remark. "I'm in the mood to celebrate."

"Sorry, I can't," said Neville. "I've got court in the morning."

"I have to be leaving too," MacKenzie added. "I'm heading on down to Belle Glade tonight."

They all shook hands again. Then Terry was walking down the wide marble stairway at Ben's side, past the rotunda and its snack shop, out into the sweet-smelling night air.

Without doubt, Terry thought, the rest of the station crew was now aware that her relationship with Ben had gone beyond a mere cessation of hostilities. There would be a lot of gossip, with correspondingly fewer opportunities to sneak off in each other's company.

At the bottom of the courthouse portico, she could feel Ben stiffen beside her. There, Larsen, his foreman and attorney were standing together in a tightly knit group.

"All you smart-aleck scientists think you've made a fool of me, don't you?" Larsen asked bitterly. "Well, I don't aim to give up yet, not by a long shot. I've got friends in Tallahassee too."

No one said anything for a minute. "This isn't a personal fight as far as we're concerned," Ben said quietly. "We're just trying to do what we think is right for the environment."

"Hell, you ain't satisfied with the big chunk of land my daddy left you to chase after birds and butterflies. You want part of what he left me, too. I always planned a subdivision on that piece of ground, and I'm gonna have it. If not, I'll graze it down to the soil come October." He turned and wagged his finger at Janet. "See that *she* keeps off my land," he added, "or you're going to find out what trouble is."

It was Arch who put a protective arm around Janet this time. Larsen and his party got into the big white Cadillac parked illegally at the curb, and drove away with a little screech of the tires that was like a final retort.

"I think he means business about that," Dave said to Janet. "I want you to observe the boundary line, do you understand?"

She nodded, the tension of being singled out showing in her face. Arch gave her a squeeze. "Don't let Larsen get you down," he said. "C'mon, folks. I remember hearing something about a drinking bout at one of the local emporiums. Shall we go?"

This time, Arch piled in with Dave's party, leaving Terry alone with Ben for the short trip to the bar.

"I guess I shouldn't have kissed you like that," Ben said, resting a hand on her knee as they paused for a red light. "I'd like us to move in together, but the truth is, we're in an awkward situation, darling."

"Yes," she said. "I know."

He didn't reply, though she had the feeling he was refraining with some difficulty from saying what was on his mind. She was still wondering about it when the six of them crowded into an oversized corner booth at the bar they had chosen. Maybe he, too, wanted to resume their long-since-aborted marriage plans, but was reluctant to broach the subject for fear of sidetracking her career. Or, she thought regretfully, he might not be thinking of anything like that. Maybe what had happened six years ago had changed him, so that he wanted just what he said and nothing more: for them to move in together. Maybe he didn't trust her any further than that.

Well, I'll take what I can get, she decided, as the waitress brought their drinks. Even to have him that way, as a clandestine lover, is more than I'd hoped for.

Almost immediately, Arch asked her to dance and she agreed gracefully, sliding out of the booth as if dancing with him were what would please her most in the world. She was happy to see that Ben asked Janet. At the moment, the blond zoology student needed a mark of favor from someone in authority at the station.

Soon, though, as if it were something they couldn't avoid, Ben and Terry found themselves dancing in each other's arms to a slow and plaintive country and western tune.

"Holding you like this makes me want to make love to you," Ben whispered, drawing her as close as he dared in that company. "It's been more than a week since we've been together like that. I should have ravished you at the fire tower that night."

"I wish now you had," said Terry. "But it wasn't the right moment."

"I know." His hand, firm against the small of her back, pressed her against him. "Maybe I'll invade your little room tonight," he murmured, "the way I used to do."

But he didn't come and she hadn't really expected him to. She lay awake a long time, tense with wanting him. Outside her window, the moon was nearly at the full. It spilled a path of shadows and silver across her bed.

Well, you know what they say about a full moon, she thought. It makes you crazy. It's going to be a rough couple of days. She couldn't wait until Thursday when she and Ben would set off for his convention in St. Petersburg Beach, then drive on down to Sanibel for three more glorious days alone.

Maybe he'll want us to take separate cars, she added to herself as she turned and plumped up her pillow. So no one will suspect. I wish for once we could be open about what we feel.

The next day her half-serious musings about the moon proved to be devastatingly accurate. The morning began quietly enough. At breakfast, everyone—including Ben—seemed vaguely irritable and out-of-sorts as they all sat around the long dining table in what had once been Olaf Larsen's garden room. It was as if they had *lost* their first hearing on the zoning question instead of winning it, Terry remarked to herself.

After a morning spent in the field, they were no less taciturn at lunch. It struck her as she ate her tuna salad sandwich and glanced at the collection of artifacts amassed by Olaf Larsen that his son Victor had plenty to be angry about. I don't suppose this is the only home his father owned, she thought. But it was the place where Victor Larsen spent a lot of time when he was growing up. The fact that he doesn't understand its special ecological character or respect it is entirely beside the point. I wish he could have inherited a little of his father's generous spirit.

Just then, Ben stood up and excused himself from the table. For the past week, she knew, he had been spending every moment not devoted to the zoning question in putting the finishing touches to his monograph. Writing an adequate finish to it concerned him, and she wasn't surprised at his abrupt, distracted manner.

Like Terry, Janet seemed to have no appetite. She also finished quickly and headed back to the Lake Annie tract to look for fresh panther tracks. It's all so anticlimactic, Terry thought—dull, in truth. I don't even want to work today. All I can think about is Ben and wanting to be alone with him so that we can show each other our love.

Yet Bob had returned early that morning from Miami, and he, at least, was eager to get back into the field. Terry supposed she would have to go too. She could hardly just snooze and lie around, waiting for the weekend.

Despite her mood, she became engrossed as soon as she began working, as fascinated with the jays' private world as a god spying on a race of mortals. I really love this work, she thought. Even if I weren't in love with Ben, being here would give me the deepest pleasure. The fact that Ben shares my interest only adds to that pleasure, and deepens my love for him. How I wish we could both have our work and each other, the way I want.

She had worked her way back into a tangle of palmetto and scrub oak when she heard the Jeep's horn honking out on the fire road. She could barely make out Arch with her binoculars. He was standing up behind the wheel and waving frantically. "Come quick, Terry!" he yelled.

She crashed through the bushes, scratching up her arms and legs in the process. "What is it?" she screamed back at him. "What's wrong?"

"Didn't you hear the gunshot?"

She scrambled into the Jeep beside Bob and hung on for dear life while Arch skidded through the rutted sand. Suddenly she recalled the sound, a distant report she had thought was the backfire of an automobile on Route 27. Now, she realized it had come from the wrong direction.

"Lake Annie?" she asked.

He nodded.

Oh, my God, she thought. Janet's gone and gotten herself killed over that panther. Please . . . don't let it be so.

They took the same combination of lurching, jolting tracks she and Ben had followed the first morning they'd gone out into the field together, the morning of Janet's run-in with Cavendish. It was a nightmare ride, seemingly in slow motion.

The sight at the fence line made Terry's heart skip a beat. Janet had scaled the fence and was standing on the Larsen side, her face white but defiant, while Cavendish held a shotgun pointed dead center at her chest.

"I told you to get back over that fence before I call the police," he said, pulling back the release on the trigger. "I'm gonna count to ten. . . ."

To Terry's incredulity, Janet refused. "This is a citizen's arrest," she said, her voice shaking. "What you tried to do is illegal."

Implacably, Cavendish began counting. "Janet!" Terry cried. "For God's sake! Do what he tells you."

She ran forward to the fence, stumbling on the uneven ground even as she heard another vehicle pull up behind them. A moment later, Ben was pushing her out of the way, going over the fence himself. *No,* she thought, *oh no!* as Arch came up beside her and tightly grabbed her hand.

Cavendish turned his gun on Ben. "You keep out of this," he said. "You're trespassing, same as her. Get back over that fence."

"Not until you put that gun down. I'm not going to let you shoot one of our students just because she set foot on your land." He paused. "I've heard one shot already."

"He was shooting at the panther, Ben." Janet's voice had steadied a little. "I *saw* him, and he was so beautiful. And then he just sailed over the fence and the shot rang out. . . ."

"You saw the panther?"

Terry's eyes widened. How could they stand there discussing this so calmly while Cavendish curled his fingers around the trigger? But even Larsen's foreman had forgotten to resume his count.

"Yes." The blond zoologist faced Ben with tears in her eyes. "I wasn't going to follow him, though I thought my heart would burst," she added. "But when *he* . . ." She pointed at the foreman with a quivering finger. "When he shot at him, I couldn't help . . ."

"I understand," said Ben tersely. "Get over the fence. Now."

She did his bidding without a word and was enfolded by Terry and Arch on the other side. But Ben was still on Larsen land, looking down the muzzle of a shotgun.

"You too," said Cavendish angrily, squinting at him. "Over."

On the verge of panic, Terry sensed that the foreman saw himself losing a third battle with the hated biologists, and with Ben in particular. His wounded pride would make him all the more dangerous.

Perhaps Ben sensed it too. "All right," he said. "Take it easy. I'm going." He took one step backward, then added perversely, "But she's right, you know, about shooting panthers. Punishable by a five-hundred-dollar fine. I guess I don't have to tell you that."

Terry held her breath as he turned his back on Cavendish and began to walk slowly, deliberately toward them. His hand was on the fencepost; he was about to climb over when the foreman aimed his weapon again.

"Ben!" Terry screamed. "Look out!"

He didn't dive or freeze. Instead he wheeled, his voice hoarse with fury, as if some boundary of reason

155

had been crossed. "So you'd shoot me in the back, would you? Why don't you put down that gun and fight like a man?"

Nonplussed by Ben's coolness, Cavendish hesitated.

"Coward," said Ben softly, as if reason indeed had flown.

Cavendish reddened. "If it's a fight you want, you'll get it," he replied suddenly, tossing the shotgun behind him in the direction of his truck. "Come and get me."

Terry's heart began to thump against her ribs as the two men began to circle each other. Cavendish was at least ten years older than Ben, but heavier, much heavier, a great bull of a man. He's going to kill Ben, Terry thought in despair. He doesn't need a gun to do that.

A second later, the two of them were grappling and she heard the sickening sound of knuckles smashing into flesh. Ben staggered backward, thrown off-balance by Cavendish's greater weight, his lip split open and bleeding. Only Arch's hand, locked around her wrist, kept her from going to him.

Ben wiped his mouth with the back of his hand.

"Come on, pretty-boy biologist," Cavendish jeered at him. "You wanted to fight me. Let's get it over with."

"Don't worry," said Ben grimly. "I intend to." Stepping now with the grace of a cat—a big cat like Janet's panther—he moved in on the foreman again. He took another punch to the face before grasping Cavendish by the arm and flipping him around so that his arm was pinned behind him. "Karate," he said. "Brown belt. U.S. Navy. Quit while you're ahead."

Cavendish laughed and wrenched himself away. "All the pretty boys say that," he taunted.

The next minute he had been tossed over Ben's

shoulder and was lying in the dirt, the wind knocked out of him. Ben picked up the shotgun, emptied out the shells and put them in his pocket. "See you later," he said, walking back to the fence, quickly now. "Don't shoot at any more panthers or I'll come looking for you."

Terry broke free and ran to him as he climbed over onto station property. "Don't," he said, as she started to put her arms around him. "C'mon. Let's get out of here."

Ben had brought Dave's truck out, and she got back in it beside him while Janet took her place in the Jeep. Without wasting words or motion, he started up the engine, turned the truck around and shot off down the fire road. An ugly bruise was starting to darken his left cheekbone.

"Ben," she said, putting one hand on his arm. "Darling, he might have killed you."

"No." He shook his head, keeping his eyes on the road. "He just wanted to bully someone, win a round at this stupid game."

"It didn't look that way to me."

He threw her a glance. "Another thing," he said. "Don't put your arms around me like that in public."

She felt her cheeks redden and withdrew her hand. "You did it the other night," she said in a small voice.

"That was a mistake. So is the fact that you're riding back with me instead of with someone else. People are talking about us already, and I have no idea if—"

He broke off in midsentence and did not rephrase or complete his thought. A minute or two later they were pulling up at the veranda in front of the lab.

Burning with anger and humiliation, she got out swiftly and started to walk away. His voice followed her. "Terry," he said, softening the hard edge of his words a little, "get me a styptic pencil and an ice bag from the medicine chest upstairs, will you please? And some ice?"

Get them yourself, she wanted to retort. But she couldn't. Not when she remembered his bruised cheek and bleeding lip. Sending him a narrowed glance over her shoulder, she went off to get the items he'd requested, leaving Arch and Bob and Janet to ply him with questions.

She was seething with hurt and fury over what she felt was a repudiation of their love. Quickly she climbed the stairs, feeling a million miles apart from Ben, as if she were a liability to him, not the object of his desire. I'll show him I can be as cool about this as he, she thought as she snatched up the ice bag and styptic pencil, then went down to the kitchen for the ice.

When she returned, Ben was alone in the lab. He had washed up in one of the sinks and was wincing as he applied peroxide to his lip.

"Thanks," he said briefly, touching the styptic to his cut and setting the ice bag aside momentarily on the counter. The bruise on his cheek was going to be nothing short of spectacular. Terry stood by quietly, watching him, unaware just how much the hostility she was feeling was showing in her face.

For a moment he returned her wordless regard. "Terry, you look awful," he said finally. "What's wrong?"

She didn't answer him immediately. How I love you, she thought—blue eyes and frowning brows, arrogant nose and a mouth that can send me into rapture. I can't let you see how much it hurts when you tell me not to touch you.

But she was still angry too. Keeping her composure,

she managed just the merest of smiles. "I was going to say the same thing to you."

He shrugged. "Oh, this. It isn't so bad. Sweetheart, I was awfully brusque with you back there."

Her jaw tightened a little. "As a matter of fact, you were. But you made your point."

Ben shook his head faintly. "People are looking at us sideways already," he said. "And it would be a disaster if word got out that we were actually having an affair. Your assistantship would be canceled. As for my job . . ."

His voice trailed off as he held the compress aside and gingerly tested his lip for further bleeding. There was none.

"Well?" Abandoning all pretense of coolness, she flung the word at him like a challenge. "What about your precious job?"

"It matters to me." Returning the compress to his jaw, he sat down in the swivel chair at his desk and looked at her from beneath slightly lowered lashes. "Maybe I was presuming too much. But I thought you felt the same way about your work."

Terry's eyes glittered dangerously. "Of course I care about it!" she exclaimed, stung. All too readily, the memory of past taunts sprang to mind. "I know what you're insinuating . . . that I have never had any real commitment to science . . . that I came back here for the sole purpose of rekindling our love affair!"

A muscle twitched alongside his mouth. "Did you?"

She recoiled from the question as if from a slap. "Maybe that was part of it," she raged, wanting to strike out at him in return. "So what if it was? I'm not ashamed of the way I feel. I came back for the project too, because it was my father's, and because I want to make this my career. Whether or not you believe it, that career means a great deal to me. I just happen to think love is more important than any job. And that it isn't love when a job means so much to you that you won't acknowledge the way you feel."

Terry was breathless from her tirade. She glared at him, her eyes flashing with hurt and righteous anger. Meanwhile, Ben was ominously quiet. "So you think I don't really love you," he said thoughtfully at last.

"Not in the way I need!"

Heedless of his tone, she tried to brush past him to the lab's sliding glass doors. But she should have known he wouldn't let her go that easily. Almost before she knew what was happening, Ben was on his feet, catching her roughly by the wrist and wheeling her about to face him.

"And that is?" he inquired, his voice raspy now with his effort to control his emotions.

Terry was on the verge of tears. "Being able to touch you if I want," she admitted, furious at the quaver she couldn't hide. "Follow you with my eyes. Show that it matters to me when someone hurts you."

With that, she turned her face aside to wipe her eyes with the heel of her hand. She didn't see the way he closed his own eyes tightly for a moment as if her frank statement and the deep caring it had revealed had pierced his defenses. And so she stiffened a little when he put both arms around her and pulled her up against him.

"What else?" he prodded in that same throaty whisper. "Sleep with me here? Even if everyone knows what's going on?"

In a saner moment, Terry would have realized how far she had pushed him and would have known better than to give an affirmative reply. But she was still feeling very vulnerable and angry indeed.

"Maybe so!" she exclaimed, twisting a little in his grasp though she was firmly held prisoner there. "Maybe that's just what I require—a man who isn't ruled by public opinion!"

For a moment she thought he would slap her, or let her go. He did neither. "All right," he said, his face inches from hers, his voice still low and deliberate though the emotional quality of it was very clear. "We'll do it your way. I just hope you don't decide to leave me again after they kick us both out of here."

11

~~~~~~~~~~~~~~~

Leave you? Terry wanted to ask, her mind spinning. *Is that what you think I'd do?* But before she could phrase a denial, Ben's mouth had come down on hers with the force of an avalanche. His tongue, rough instrument of his own anger and passion, had forced her lips apart. To her horror, she could taste the faint salty tang of his blood.

"Ben," she breathed, pitting her lesser strength against his as she tried to draw back a little. "Your lip is bleeding again."

"It isn't serious." The words were muffled as he went on kissing her, invading her will and smothering all protest. His strong, beautiful hands were molding her to the shape of his body as if somehow her bones could melt into his.

A welter of conflicting emotions battled for the upper hand as Terry's palms cradled the broad muscles of his shoulders. She felt half adversary and half lover in his arms. Angry still, she knew she was responding nonetheless to the magnetic pull of him, even as common sense set off alarms in her head.

Here, right here in the lab where someone could walk in on them at any moment, Ben had abandoned all caution and show of propriety. What he was doing could earn him a reprimand, she knew. It could lose him the respect of his colleagues and other students, maybe even get him fired as he had suggested.

Not to mention getting her thrown off the project. I don't want either of those things to happen, she thought desperately, any more than I want us to keep on pretending.

As if he could sense her inner conflict, he pulled her closer still, crushing her breasts against the sweat- and dirt-stained front of his shirt. Perhaps intent on demonstrating just how far he was prepared to go, he slipped one hand into the back of her shorts.

"No," she managed. "Not here. . . ."

He brushed her protest aside. "I thought this was what you wanted," he returned hoarsely. "What we feel for each other out in the open. No secrets. I'll show you how much I love you, since you're fool enough to doubt it."

One hand tangled in the short blond curls at her nape, he tilted her head back so that he might swoop down again to plunder her mouth. She had a sudden realization of what would happen if she were unable to stop him. Blunt and passionate when pushed beyond the limits of his formidable control, he was capable of making love to her right there amid the lab reports and Bunsen burners.

"Ben, for God's sake," she begged. "This isn't what I wanted."

"Isn't it?" His mouth punished hers again. "Tell me the truth. It's been more than a week since we've made love. Tell me you don't want us to be together like that."

Terry felt herself go hot all over with what he was proposing. Somehow, she had to resist, to fight herself as she was fighting him, for both their sakes.

"We . . . might as well do it on the dining porch," she blurted out, clutching at humor in a desperate attempt to curb him. "Really give them something to talk about when they come in to dinner."

Her salvo went wide of its mark. Fire leaped wickedly in his blue eyes even as his mouth curved faintly, revealing that her words had only ignited his imagination. "Would you like that, darling girl?" he murmured, kissing her again. "Because if you would . . ."

Outside, on the veranda, there were footsteps. A moment later, the lab door rolled back and Arch walked in. "By any chance have you seen our charts?" he began. "Bob swears he left them in here. . . ."

Then he fell silent as he registered what was happening. Though they had drawn apart a little at the intrusion, Ben continued to hold Terry firmly by the waist. It would have been impossible for an idiot to mistake what was going on, and Arch was far from that. Terry felt herself go crimson as she returned his stare.

"I think I saw them in Bob's lab carrel," Ben said evenly.

Arch gave him a blank look.

"The lab reports," Ben reminded.

"Oh. Yeah, thanks." Tearing his eyes from the two of them with obvious effort, Arch hurried to collect the sheaf of papers he was seeking from Bob's study area.

"I need to talk to him a moment," Ben told Terry in an aside. "Wait for me upstairs."

"In my room?" She put the incredulous question in a whisper, unwilling for Arch to overhear.

Ben raised one brow. "Why not? It'll be all over the station now anyway."

So he wasn't going to ask Arch to keep his mouth shut. Instead he was going to "go public" the way he had threatened to do, and let matters take their course.

Without a word she turned and walked out, too embarrassed even to say hello to Janet who was sitting on the far end of the veranda, near the carpentry shop. What I need is a drive, she thought, a chance to get away for a couple of hours and think.

She knew she would have to be quick. The keys to the MG were upstairs in the night table beside her bed, and Ben would be detained with Arch for only a few minutes at best. She didn't want to meet him coming back down the stairs and cause a scene.

Breaking into a run, she took the stairs to the sleeping quarters two at a time. Her keys were in the drawer as she had remembered, atop the diary that she had been rereading little by little in recent weeks. On impulse she snatched it up too and raced out, leaving the door to her room ajar. There was no sign of Ben as she sprinted around the tangle of Brazilian pepper that separated the main station building from the garage and parking area.

Out of the corner of her eye she saw the lab door open. Ben was coming out with Arch as the MG shot down the asphalt drive and turned east toward the gates. There was no doubt that he had seen her. She could only imagine what Arch must have been thinking at that moment.

As she crossed U.S. 27 and started up the bumpy track to the Red Hill fire tower, it occurred to her that Ben might guess her destination and follow. Well, if he does, I'll deal with that, she thought. It'll be better than confronting him right now at the station. Still, she hoped he would let her go for that afternoon, at least, so that she could straighten out her thoughts.

Ben's friend from the Forest Service came out at the approach of an unfamiliar car, then recognized her and waved her by. "Where's Ben?" he called after her. "You can't get much smooching done up here by yourself."

She forced a bright smile. "Working," she replied, parking the convertible beside his truck. "I'm playing hookey, as you've probably guessed."

He grinned. "I won't tell. Congratulations on winning that zoning thing. You all worked mighty hard on that."

"Thanks. It meant a lot to us. But we aren't home free yet, you know. There's still the commission ruling to come and lobbying the state to designate the area a public wilderness."

"If anybody can do it, you all can." With another wave, he stepped back inside.

Grateful to end the cheerful little exchange, she hiked up the hill as she and Ben had done the night they'd gotten the news about Mike. The cabin was nearing completion, she saw, though it wasn't occupied yet. Sunlight dappled the wooden deck where they had lain together under the stars. She noted the fresh smell of the pines.

It's true what I told the forest ranger, she thought to herself, sitting down with her legs dangling over the edge of the wooden platform. Lake Annie and the preservation of the wilderness out here do mean a lot—to both of us. And so does the project. Maybe there are other unique places fragile and threatened enough to warrant doing battle for them, other species Ben could study to complete his research on communal breeding patterns. But he is committed to this place and this species, just as my father was. The home that he loves is nearby. Years of his life are invested here—the same years he spent without me. I have no right to come back now and selfishly ask that he put me first.

Yet that was exactly what she had done, and now he seemed determined to risk everything just to prove a point. It was a risk she couldn't let him take. Not if she loved him. Anyway, his work was his life. Even if she were willing to deprive him of his career, she knew its loss would ultimately drive them apart.

Still, to go back to the arm's-length affair they had been conducting was unthinkable, even if Ben would agree to that. At first, being reunited with him had been enough, but now she wanted more. How can I go on acting as if we're just colleagues or casual friends? she asked herself with a faint shake of her head. It hurts too much for us to be that separate.

Well, if you quit the program you could be his lover and not jeopardize his career, one part of herself argued. Marry him if he asked you. Live with him at the beach and keep house for him in one of the cottages at the station.

But she knew that kind of thinking wouldn't do. Never mind that he wouldn't respect her for it. The real catch was that she wouldn't respect herself. Whatever the outcome, her career would never be shelved again. I do care about being a scientist, she admitted softly, every bit as much as Ben is hoping I do.

Somewhere in the pine branches a mockingbird trilled as Terry stretched out her tanned, bare legs and absently inspected her worn tennis shoes. Why couldn't life be simple? she wondered. The way it had been when they'd swum so deliciously together at his Sanibel house, their bare skin touching in the surf, or the night before, when they had drifted to sleep in each other's arms with the breeze ruffling the curtains.

No one could be as tender and cherishing as Ben had been in those stolen moments, and it had seemed then that there could be no obstacle to their love. Now she felt as if all her reasoning was circular. They were damned no matter which course they chose. *I love him too much to spoil his career,* she thought. *Or my own. And I know my own limitations. I won't be able to go on as we have been.*

The diary she had caught up from her bedside table at the station lay beside her hand on the wooden decking, and Ben's drugstore postcard with the bathing beauty and the oranges slid out as she picked it up. Thoughtfully she turned the card over, reading his scrawled message once again. *"Leave me never,"* he had written, too late to prevent her from walking out of his life. If she hadn't, she would have her doctorate already and they would be married now. There would be no quandary to face.

Losing him a second time because she wouldn't settle for half of what she wanted would nearly kill her, she knew. Still, she let a bleak new idea intrude into her thoughts. Perhaps it would be better to go somewhere far from Larsen Park to study, where she would have a professor who could fire only her intellect, not her heart.

When Terry returned to the station just before the supper hour, she still didn't have any answers. She didn't meet Ben as she went upstairs to wash, and she wondered if he had gone off on his own to think, as she had.

But he had not. She had barely taken her seat when he came in the door and walked around to stand behind her chair.

"Your nose got sunburned this afternoon," he said,

laying one hand warmly on her shoulder in a way the others couldn't mistake. "Where did you go . . . up to Red Hill?"

So he had guessed and had elected to give her the space she needed. "As a matter of fact, I did," she said. "Your friend George said to congratulate you on winning the zoning question. I told him we still had a lot of work to do."

"You were right." Giving her shoulder a little squeeze, he took the chair beside her, for all the world as if they had been a couple for years.

Glancing at Arch, Terry got a faint but friendly nod before he looked away. It saddened her a little to realize he probably wouldn't flirt with her again or ask her to the movies now that he knew how things stood. But his brief nod had contained understanding and acceptance too, and for that she was grateful.

Of course Dave, who was deep in discussion with Janet about some problems that had cropped up on her bobcat project, knew the whole story and had quietly tendered his support. But there was something prim, almost conservative, about Janet, and Bob Dawes was an unknown quantity. We might not be so lucky with either of them, she thought.

Over dessert, Ben asked her to spend some time with him in the lab that evening, going over the final draft of the speech he would give the following afternoon in St. Petersburg Beach. As if he had guessed her thoughts about Arch, he brought up the subject the minute they were alone.

"I suppose you've been wondering what I wanted to speak to Arch about this afternoon," he remarked as he opened the lab door and stood aside for her to pass. "I don't know if you realized that he asked me earlier this week about coming with us this weekend. I told him

169

how I feel about you and explained that we needed the time alone."

His directness surprised her. "What . . . did he say?"

Ben shrugged and flipped on the fluorescent lights. "That it was okay, he understood. Also that he's fond of you and wants you to be happy."

For the second time that evening, Terry felt a tug of affection for her friend. "Arch is pretty special," she said. "He won't cast any aspersions. Besides, we're taking care of that ourselves."

Ben didn't take the bait and it seemed that the subject of their argument that afternoon was closed. They settled down to work. Seated at one of the carrels, Terry went over the pages that had already been typed, looking for errors and checking to make sure each sentence could be read smoothly aloud.

Again she noted the clear turn of phrase, the elegance of argument that had characterized his portion of the book he'd written with Avery Wilder. "You're really going to impress them with this," she said suddenly, breaking the silence. "It's wonderful, you know."

From his desk, where he was putting the finishing touches on his conclusion, Ben looked up at her and grinned. "Thanks," he said, taking off his glasses for a moment. "I hope so. In the academic game, your reputation is everything, and that book I wrote with Avery didn't help very much, I'm afraid."

Nor will our love affair, she rejoined silently as she went back to work. I can't let you undo everything that means so much to you. Yet, even at that moment, she could feel the love they shared as a tangible thing between them. Without Ben, her life would be as empty as the six years she had lived in Chicago as Philip's wife. You'd better be sure you can't handle patience and discretion before you do anything foolish, her inner self warned. He'd never forgive you if you left him again.

It was almost midnight by the time they had finished retyping the manuscript and photocopying it in the station library. The TV room was deserted. Apparently, everyone else had gone to bed.

To Terry, their footsteps echoed tellingly on the stairs that led to the sleeping quarters, alerting Arch and Bob in their room across from hers that she and Ben had come up together. As for Ben, he hadn't alluded to the unresolved issues between them even once that evening. Just the same, she had a fair idea of what he would do when they reached the darkened hall.

She wasn't mistaken. As they halted outside her door, his arms came around her. "Terry," he whispered close to her ear. "I need you, sweetheart. Let me sleep with you tonight."

There was none of the hard insistence that had edged his voice that afternoon. Still she panicked a little, because of their surroundings. "Ben, hush!" she pleaded. "They'll hear. You know we can't do what you're suggesting."

"I thought that was what you wanted," he said, referring to their afternoon conversation.

Lovingly, reasonably, he lowered his dark head to reinforce the observation with a kiss. She found his warm probing of her mouth a difficult argument to overcome. As usual, just the feel of him and his scent in her nostrils were sweeping all caution aside.

And her answering need for him at that moment was great. More than anything, she wanted him in her little room, in her bed, filling her with the glorious essence of him and making skyrockets explode in the night.

Yet she was acutely aware of the listening quality of

the silence and the danger to Ben that it represented. Maybe Arch wouldn't gossip, but she couldn't count on Bob Dawes. If he were to mention what he'd heard when they returned to Tampa in the fall . . .

"Darling, I can't let you," she said.

He kissed her again. "Don't you love me?"

"You'll never know how much. But we can't talk about it here in the hall. . . ."

"Then invite me in."

"No. Ben, please."

"I want to prove to you that I love you."

"Then let things be tonight." She touched his mouth lightly with her fingertips. "There's been a lot said today. We both need some time to let things settle."

He was silent a moment. "All right," he said. "You're coming with me tomorrow, aren't you, to St. Petersburg and down to the beach for the weekend?"

Her hesitation was barely perceptible. "Yes," she agreed. "I'm coming with you."

At that he kissed her again, a more demanding kiss, as if he were affixing his stamp of ownership. "Then I'd better let you get some sleep," he murmured, keeping his voice low, though she feared it wasn't low enough. "I guarantee you aren't going to get much of that for the next four days."

"Ben . . ."

She could feel him grinning at her, there in the dark. "An added warning," he said. "I want to be on the road by eight o'clock. If you don't rouse your beautiful body out of bed on time, I'll be coming in to get you. Appearances be damned."

To her surprise, she fell into sleep like a pebble sinking through clear water, awakening only when her alarm rang at seven the next morning. She could remember no dreams as she showered and wriggled into her slip and underwear.

She was startled by a knock on her door. "Don't dress up, sweetheart," Ben called. "We're taking the Jeep and we can put the top down. I'll be in the lab when you're ready to go."

Removing the slip again, she folded it and put it, with her white linen suit and heliotrope silk blouse, into her smallest suitcase. Probably we'll look like a couple of beach bums checking in, she thought, stepping into white shorts instead and tying on a light blue halter. But she knew Ben was right—the morning was humid already and promised a summery, perhaps even scorching day.

Adding several more pairs of shorts and a couple of bikinis for their stay on Sanibel, she snapped the case shut and started downstairs. He had pulled the Jeep up to the edge of the veranda. I'm really going away with him and everyone knows it, she thought, half-amazed at their daring as she stashed her case behind the seat.

Yet her mind refused either to plan the pleasures of their time together or to confront directly the issue of what a flagrant affair might ultimately mean to their careers. For a moment, she just stood there, her hand resting on the Jeep's roll bar, listening to a pine warbler's trill, her mind almost bereft of thought.

"Terry . . ." Ann Nesbitt was calling her name.

"Yes?" She half turned toward the housekeeper, trying not to let the expression on her face add to the evidence of her single piece of luggage beside Ben's suit bag and duffel.

Ann didn't seem to notice anything out of the ordinary. "There's someone on the phone for Ben," she said. "Long distance. I rang down in the lab and got a busy signal. If you're going down that way, maybe you could ask him to pick up on nine-two."

"Sure. No problem."

"And have a good weekend." Ann ducked back into the dining porch, probably to resume clearing away breakfast.

Terry bumped into Ben at the lab door and gave him the message, then waited outside at his request while he took the long-distance call. A few minutes later they were off, with Ben behind the wheel though she offered to drive so he could collect his thoughts.

"I need something to do with my hands," he said with a grin, shifting gears and then curling his fingers affectionately into the hair at her nape. There was a happy, almost excited tone in his voice that she hadn't heard since the night of the zoning hearing. He really loves this kind of thing, she concluded. It means even more to him than I thought.

"Who was that on the phone?" she asked as they turned at the light onto Route 70.

"The first call was Abby," he said, and then added at her swift glance, "Nothing upsetting. I'll tell you about it . . . *and* the other call . . . later, when the time is right."

Terry glanced at him curiously. What was he up to? But it was a beautiful morning, one to smooth away uncertainties. Gradually she allowed herself to settle into it, forgetting any difficult decisions that might have to be made and just enjoying the faultless sky, the air wafting heavy with citrus blooms, a light breeze whipping at their hair.

Almost before she knew it, they were passing through Bradenton and crossing the incredibly high span of the Skyway Bridge, above the hammered silver expanse of Tampa Bay. Then they were turning west near the

Eckerd College campus, toward the Gulf. She could see the hotel from a distance. Huge, old-fashioned and Spanish, it stood there on the beach like an enormous pink wedding cake, just as Ben had described it.

The sound of water splashing from a fountain provided a musical, almost Moorish accent as Ben registered at the tiled front desk. Terry waited, feeling gauche and a bit too bare-legged beside some of the more soberly dressed conference participants who were arriving with their suitably academic husbands and wives.

There was a moment of acute embarrassment for her as Ben nodded hello to two of the men as he picked up their key. To her chagrin, he proceeded to introduce her as his student, and one of the men gave her a thorough looking over from head to toe.

She forgot about the awkward moment, at least temporarily, when Ben grabbed her inside their room and tugged her down with him onto the king-sized bed.

"We're here," he exulted, pressing his body down on hers. "Away from the madding crowd. Just me and my beautiful girl. This weekend"—he interspersed a kiss— "I'm going to show you . . . and *show* you . . . just how much you're loved."

The weight of him, so sweet after too much separateness, that mossy musk aroma of his that filled her nostrils like an aphrodisiac, the texture of his hair against her cheek as he nuzzled her neck—surely these delights should have shaped the moment. Why then did some nameless fear seem to settle against her heart?

"Hold me, Ben," she whispered, gathering him painfully close. "All I want you to do is hold me."

12

More than that, my sweet love.''

Laughing, Ben rolled off her and headed for the shower, urging her to have a swim first, before his speech at two o'clock. He himself would dress and go downstairs to prowl about, see which big names in the scientific community had arrived for the conference, and get himself in the right frame of mind for his presentation.

Sensing that he needed the time alone, she did as he suggested, lolling in the gulfside pool, listening to the Latin beat of a mariachi group, and sipping two margarita cocktails that went quite powerfully to her head in the hot sun. Despite the drinks, she was not able to drive her apprehension away.

At one-thirty, she donned the white suit, making up her large brown eyes with a heliotrope shadow to match her blouse. Carefully she stroked on mascara. For once, she wanted to look sleek and sophisticated for the man she loved.

She slipped into a seat near the back of the auditorium just as Ben was introduced. How powerful and masculine and self-assured he looked in a gray pinstripe suit she had never seen, how unruffled by the meagerness of the applause that greeted him as he took the podium.

At first, she was lost in appreciation of his speech and the polished way he delivered it, even though by this time she knew nearly every word of it by heart. Then her attention was riveted by a whispered exchange just in front of her, between the two men Ben had greeted briefly in the lobby that morning.

" . . . nubile, I'd call her," one of them was saying, in tones that doubtless carried farther than he had intended. "A good-looking rear and great legs. He's got a lot of gall, though, bringing her here. Five'll get you ten they're registered as man and wife."

The other man shrugged, annoyed perhaps that he was missing part of the talk. "What did you expect, Harry? After that book he wrote with Wilder, I'm not at all surprised by anything Reno might do."

Behind them, Terry went cold all over, as if she were in shock. Shaking, she managed to extricate herself from the row of chairs and stumble from the room.

The hall outside was nearly deserted and she halted, her hands covering her face. Somehow, she had to regain control. Willing herself to regain her calm, she stared out an arching wall of windows toward the turquoise Gulf and the hotel pool where she'd had her margaritas less than an hour before.

Huge tears slipped down her cheeks. What have I done? she asked herself despairingly. Oh my God, what have I done to him?

"Everything okay, miss?" One of the bellhops was giving her an inquiring, sympathetic look. With his red hair, he reminded her of Arch.

"I'm . . . all right." Ineffectually she dabbed at her eyes. "Or will be, in a moment. I . . . just need to go upstairs."

She could feel him following her with his eyes as she made her way to the elevators. I've got to get out of here, she thought numbly, before Ben finishes. I don't want to spoil his triumph.

The hotel room mocked her with its lingering air of intimacy—the rumpled imprint of their bodies on the spread, Ben's duffel bag standing open on a chair. Just the way those men imagined it, she thought. A professor and a student carrying on an affair. I can't do this to him.

Somehow, she managed to change into her halter top and shorts again. Stepping out of the elevator into the main-floor lobby, she saw Ben emerging from the ballroom at the far end of the hall. Members of the audience were crowding around him, offering handshakes and congratulations. Even at that distance, she could see his distracted look. She realized that he had seen her go out. He would be looking for her.

Not yet, Terry hedged. I have to think.

Backing into the elevator again, she collided with a beefy man in swimming trunks. "Make up your mind, lady," he muttered, pushing past her.

Clutching her key, she rode on down to the terrace and pool level. The South American music with its marimba beat, the chatter of the hotel guests and the splashing of their children didn't seem so festive now. Skirting the holiday crowd, Terry struck out down the beach toward Pass-a-Grille.

Certain she had eluded Ben, at least for the moment, that he would not look for her immediately among the sunbrowned tourists on the beach, she slowed her steps. She felt awash in loneliness. Ben, she wept silently, the tears spilling now that she thought herself out of reach. I don't ever want to leave you again. Yet how can I stay? I love you too much to make you an object of gossip among your colleagues.

She gave a little cry as his arms came around her, causing people to turn toward them and stare. What a sight they must make, she thought, she in her shorts and halter, with tears running down her cheeks, he upset and barefoot in his pinstripe suit.

Roughly he held her. "Where do you think you're going?" he demanded, with something that might have been fear or anger just edging his voice. "Why did you walk out on the meeting that way?"

Terry didn't know how to answer him. "I had to get out of there," she stammered. "To think."

His jaw tightened. "About what?"

Ben's hands were hurting her, digging into her arms. "It was those men," she whispered. "The ones we met in the lobby. They were talking about us . . . about you sleeping around with one of your students."

Ben swore. "And you think that matters? C'mon . . . let's go."

Probably to bystanders it appeared that he was manhandling her as he propelled her, half dragged her, back toward the hotel. Yet there was something in his eyes, something flint hard that brooked no interference, and no one stepped forward to help.

Coming up from the sand onto the pool terrace, she stumbled, nearly dropping her key, and a muscle twitched alongside his mouth as he slowed his pace a little. But he was angry still, angrier than she had ever seen him, as he punched the elevator button viciously with one tanned index finger.

Inside their room, the bright vista of the Gulf sparkled away outside the window. With an expert little jerk, he removed her halter top, tossing it aside. Almost before she knew what was happening, he was moving her backward, toward the bed, yanking off the Spanish-style woven spread to reveal the sheets.

"Lie down," he said, his voice raspy and deep. "We're going to make love."

She sat, curling up her legs. "Please, Ben," she entreated. "Not like this. . . ."

He was taking off his own things—jacket, shirt and tie. His hand paused at his belt buckle, something softening in his face. "Sweetheart," he said with just the faintest reproach. "Who do you think I'm mad at, anyway?"

Then he had removed his trousers and he was on the bed again beside her, making her lie back against the pillows, taking her in his arms. "Terry, Terry," he said, his words muffled against the softness of her breast. "Darling, you wouldn't really leave me again over something so foolish?"

"I wouldn't want to," she whispered. "Not ever. But I don't want to be the cause of embarrassment or trouble. . . ."

"Only one thing could ever really hurt me," he said.

After that, real words weren't possible. Systematically and with deliberate passion, he began to shower her skin with little kisses—eyelids, mouth, breasts, the silken tanned curve of her stomach that was revealed as he unzipped her shorts. Moans of delight escaped her.

"Help me, my beautiful girl." He nudged her shorts and bikini panties from her hips. In response, she pulled them down herself and kicked them free, shivering with longing as he pressed himself against her.

She knew the answer now, finally, to all the agonizing questions that had plagued her, as she clung to his hardness and warmth. Whatever the cost in frustration to stick things out until she got her doctorate and they were home free, she would gladly pay it. The alternative didn't even bear thinking about.

If only we can put things back the way they were, make people forget, she thought desperately. The dean will never have to know.

"Ben, oh, Ben. I was wrong to want to make a public display of things," she confessed. "But it's not too late. If we're careful, try to set things right—"

"Don't talk." He gave her a piercing, blue-eyed look before lowering his head again to her breast. "I'm trying to show you how right it will be."

They couldn't settle it now. Helplessly, she gave herself over to the sensations he was arousing, writhing beneath his touch as he licked her nipples, pushed up her breasts' fullness, the better to tug on them with his mouth. Her hands tangled in his wiry, curling hair, caressed the long muscles of his back and hips as almost unbearable pleasures pierced her to the core. She felt her inner being expand even more to receive him, as if she were a well as boundless as the world, one that only he could fill.

She was half-crazy in her need for him. "Darling, please," she begged finally, her breath coming in ragged little gasps. "I don't want to wait."

"Neither do I," he admitted hoarsely. "Neither do I." The next moment, he was coming into her, all hardness and power and strength. She gave a little wordless cry as they began to move in unison, like wrestlers with but one aim, one victory to win between them.

Ever-deepening waves of rapture washed over them as their sweet intoxication with each other mounted, waves that seemed to break with increasing frequency until they dissolved together in mutual delight.

She could feel the blood pounding through their separate bodies as if it were one stream, knew his deep, pleasurable ache of satisfaction as if it were her own. He had collapsed against her, pinning her to the bed, and she cradled him lovingly as her tremors subsided.

"I love you so much, Ben," she told him.

"I know, sweetheart. I love you too."

Several minutes later he got up to close the drapes and went into the bathroom. Then he was bringing her back a glass of water, the coldest the faucet could provide, and lying back down beside her.

"You're so beautiful, you know," he said as she sipped her drink. "Do you really think you could stand to wait until we can afford to live openly together?"

"I'll have to." Terry traced the rim of the water glass with her finger. "One thing I know for certain . . . I can't live without you. And I found out something else: it isn't fair to stack up your career against the person you love. Either way, you lose."

Ben pursed his lips slightly, as if he were hiding some secret amusement. "Then you won't try to leave me again . . . even if the tension gets tough to take?"

"No." Though she was puzzled at the lightness of his tone, the single word rang with the deepest conviction. "I'll be so patient you won't be able to stand it."

He was silent a moment and she took another sip of her water, waiting.

"I don't plan to be patient," he said finally, still with that faintly quizzical expression on his face. "And I don't intend for us just to live together, either. I intend to marry you . . . right away."

Terry almost choked. "What . . . what are you talking about?" she sputtered, handing the glass back to him. "We've been through all that already. If we get married, or even make it *look* like we're lovers, your reputation is in shreds. They won't let us work together."

"I know the whole litany. Say yes."

"But, Ben . . ."

"Say it. Maybe you haven't realized it, sweetheart, but ever since that rainy afternoon on Dave's boat, when we came home in each other's arms, marriage is what I've been thinking of. I just couldn't say anything, couldn't ask you to risk giving up the work you'd started again, when I was so proud of you."

Ben's gaze was so warm and blue and deep she thought she could drown in it. "And now?" she hazarded breathlessly. "Now you think it will be all right?"

In response, he took her back into his arms. "The second phone call this morning was from Tampa," he said. "Do you remember the other time I asked you to leave the lab so I could take a call about a student? Well, that student was you, darling, and I was begging the dean of my college to allow a special arrangement whereby we could work together but Dave would grade your efforts so that there could be no hint of favoritism. This morning I got my answer."

Terry's eyes were shining. "It was yes, wasn't it?" she exclaimed, hugging him. "Oh, Ben. It was yes."

He grinned at her, his lip still showing the cut Larsen's foreman had given him, the bruise from that same battle fading now along his cheekbone. He was still the most beautiful man in the world.

"That's all you have to say," he reminded her, lightly tracing the shape of her mouth. "One three-letter affirmative word."

"Yes," she told him as she placed a warm kiss on his fingertips. "This time it will be forever."

Later, much later, they stirred together, woke in a darkened room. Getting up, she reopened the drapes to reveal a sky deepening from orange to magenta and blue-violet. Activity on the hotel terrace had dwindled to a murmur, and even with the windows closed they could hear the *hush-hush, hush-hush* of the surf.

"Hungry?" he asked from the bed as he watched her move in silhouette against the fading light.

"Not really," she said. "Just for you."

He blew her a silent little kiss. "We could stay here tonight, or go on down to Sanibel. Say which."

"Let's go home."

Three-quarters of an hour later, they were heading south, across the bay. The top of the Jeep was still down and the noise of the rushing air made them raise their voices a little. Overhead, the sky was an inky vault already, lit by what seemed to be infinite firepoints of stars.

"You haven't asked me about Abby again," Ben said, resting his hand on her knee as he drove. "I have some news about her that might interest you."

"What news?" Terry asked.

"Mike's on the road to recovery, and he and Abby are going to try again."

"But . . . I thought . . ."

"Mike has checked into a rehabilitation unit for problem drinkers of his own free will. It seems he wrote her that he was getting out of her life for good because he wanted her to be happy. That was all it took."

"She won't let her parents ruin things for them again?"

Ben shook his head. "They have a lot of problems

yet to settle. But I don't think so. Oh, and I have one other thing to tell you. Dave got a call this morning too—from Larsen. The old boys plans to fight us tooth and nail in Tallahassee. But he assured Dave there won't be any shooting out on the Lake Annie property again."

"That's wonderful." Terry closed her eyes. "An even chance is all we need."

They rode in silence after that, a comfortable silence in which their closeness seemed to deepen, though each was lost in separate thought. *I can hardly believe it,* Terry acknowledged to herself in amazement. *But he's going to be my husband. I'll have a lifetime of his love.*

It was midnight when they pulled into Ben's driveway beneath the softly whispering coconut palms and Australian pines. Terry had slept a little on the way down and she was still drowsy as Ben unlocked the door and set the luggage inside.

"Welcome," he said as he slipped one arm about her and drew her in. "You were right this evening, you know, to call this place home. I designed it for you long ago, after you agreed to marry me the first time. I built it when I could afford to, even though by then I'd lost you. I don't know what kind of crazy hope . . ."

"Oh, *Ben.*" Overwhelmed at the way he had loved her across the years of their separation, she nestled closer in his arms. "I came back with the same hope," she whispered. "Sweetheart, we'll never hurt each other again."

In the darkened living room, the clock chimed the quarter hour. "I'm crazy about you," Ben told her. "Let's go to bed."

For Terry, the joy of the moment seemed to overflow. "I suppose we'll need our sleep if we're to get up for a nude swim before anyone's on the beach," she laughed, wanting to tease him now and loving the way his eyes gleamed suggestively at her there in the dark.

In answer, he slid one hand inside the tee shirt and sweater she wore and traced her backbone. "Sorry, darling," he said, pleasure evident in the timbre of his rough, sweet voice. "But we'll have to skinny dip some other time. I don't plan to let you out of bed that early."

YOU'LL BE SWEPT AWAY WITH SILHOUETTE DESIRE

$1.75 each

1 ☐ James
2 ☐ Monet
3 ☐ Clay
4 ☐ Carey

5 ☐ Baker
6 ☐ Mallory
7 ☐ St. Claire

8 ☐ Dee
9 ☐ Simms
10 ☐ Smith

$1.95 each

11 ☐ James
12 ☐ Palmer
13 ☐ Wallace
14 ☐ Valley
15 ☐ Vernon
16 ☐ Major
17 ☐ Simms
18 ☐ Ross
19 ☐ James
20 ☐ Allison
21 ☐ Baker
22 ☐ Durant
23 ☐ Sunshine
24 ☐ Baxter
25 ☐ James
26 ☐ Palmer
27 ☐ Conrad
28 ☐ Lovan

29 ☐ Michelle
30 ☐ Lind
31 ☐ James
32 ☐ Clay
33 ☐ Powers
34 ☐ Milan
35 ☐ Major
36 ☐ Summers
37 ☐ James
38 ☐ Douglass
39 ☐ Monet
40 ☐ Mallory
41 ☐ St. Claire
42 ☐ Stewart
43 ☐ Simms
44 ☐ West
45 ☐ Clay
46 ☐ Chance

47 ☐ Michelle
48 ☐ Powers
49 ☐ James
50 ☐ Palmer
51 ☐ Lind
52 ☐ Morgan
53 ☐ Joyce
54 ☐ Fulford
55 ☐ James
56 ☐ Douglass
57 ☐ Michelle
58 ☐ Mallory
59 ☐ Powers
60 ☐ Dennis
61 ☐ Simms
62 ☐ Monet
63 ☐ Dee
64 ☐ Milan

65 ☐ Allison
66 ☐ Langtry
67 ☐ James
68 ☐ Browning
69 ☐ Carey
70 ☐ Victor
71 ☐ Joyce
72 ☐ Hart
73 ☐ St. Clair
74 ☐ Douglass
75 ☐ McKenna
76 ☐ Michelle
77 ☐ Lowell
78 ☐ Barber
79 ☐ Simms
80 ☐ Palmer
81 ☐ Kennedy
82 ☐ Clay

YOU'LL BE SWEPT AWAY WITH SILHOUETTE DESIRE

$1.95 each

83 ☐ Chance	95 ☐ Summers	107 ☐ Chance	119 ☐ John
84 ☐ Powers	96 ☐ Milan	108 ☐ Gladstone	120 ☐ Clay
85 ☐ James	97 ☐ James	109 ☐ Simms	121 ☐ Browning
86 ☐ Malek	98 ☐ Joyce	110 ☐ Palmer	122 ☐ Trent
87 ☐ Michelle	99 ☐ Major	111 ☐ Browning	123 ☐ Paige
88 ☐ Trevor	100 ☐ Howard	112 ☐ Nicole	124 ☐ St. George
89 ☐ Ross	101 ☐ Morgan	113 ☐ Cresswell	125 ☐ Caimi
90 ☐ Roszel	102 ☐ Palmer	114 ☐ Ross	126 ☐ Carey
91 ☐ Browning	103 ☐ James	115 ☐ James	
92 ☐ Carey	104 ☐ Chase	116 ☐ Joyce	
93 ☐ Berk	105 ☐ Blair	117 ☐ Powers	
94 ☐ Robbins	106 ☐ Michelle	118 ☐ Milan	

SILHOUETTE DESIRE, Department SD/6
1230 Avenue of the Americas
New York, NY 10020

Please send me the books I have checked above. I am enclosing $_____
(please add 75¢ to cover postage and handling. NYS and NYC residents please
add appropriate sales tax). Send check or money order—no cash or C.O.D.'s
please. Allow six weeks for delivery.

NAME_____

ADDRESS_____

CITY_____STATE/ZIP_____

Coming Next Month

Fabulous Beast by Stephanie James

Before, Tabitha had only studied the elusive beasts of legend. Then she rescued Dev Colter from danger on a remote island and found that she had awakened a slumbering dragon.

Political Passions by Suzanne Michelle

Newly-elected mayor Wallis Carmichael was furious to discover that sensual Sam Davenport was really a Pulitzer Prize winning-journalist. Politics and journalism don't mix—and now she had to find out if he was just another reporter out for a story.

Madison Avenue Marriage by Cassandra Bishop

Famous mystery writer Lily Lansden needed a "husband" for her winery commercial and Trent Daily fit the bill. But when the game of pretend turned into real love could Lily give up her Madison Avenue marriage?

Between the Covers by Laurien Blair

Everything changed between co-authors Adam and Haley when they began writing their ninth book together—a romance. Were they only playing out a story or were they friends now unleashing desires restrained for too long?

To Touch the Fire by Shirley Larson

Raine had loved Jade since she was sixteen—but he was her sister's husband. Now her sister had left him—would his bitterness and her guilt over the past threaten their awakening passions?

On Love's Own Terms by Cathlyn McCoy

Luke Ford had been out of Bonnie's life for seven years. But now her devastating husband wanted a second chance, and Bonnie's common sense was betrayed by a passion that still burned.